# The LOST MEDALLION

# The LOST MEDALLION

## The Adventures of Billy Stone

B&H
KIDS

Nashville, Tennessee

Copyright © 2013 by
MeThinx Entertainment and Alex Kendrick
All rights reserved.
Printed in the United States of America

978-1-4336-8206-3

Published by B&H Publishing Group
Nashville, Tennessee

Contributing Editor: Kathryn Tedrick

Dewey Decimal Classification: JF
Subject Heading: ADVENTURE FICTION \ TIME
TRAVEL—FICTION \ PROVIDENCE AND
GOVERNMENT OF GOD—FICTION

1 2 3 4 5 6 7 8 • 17 16 15 14 13

*To John and Marilyn Duke,*
*Who have invested their life in making a difference in those less fortunate around the world.*

*The Lost Medallion* is more than just a story about two friends searching for a lost treasure. This adventure reminds us all that our significance isn't found in accomplishments, the number of friends we have, or the labels in our clothes. It reveals that our significance is found in the truth that God has created each of us with an amazing "worth and purpose" and is personally involved in our lives.

Hopefully, you will see that this is a story not so much about a "lost medallion" as it is about a "lost significance." I hope that while you are enjoying this wild adventure across an amazing island, you will also experience the powerful truths hidden within this adventure.

Sincerely,
Bill Muir

Dear Readers,

Over the last several years, I've been a cowriter and director for the films *Courageous, Fireproof,* and *Facing the Giants.* While these films were geared toward families in general, they mostly spoke to adults in particular. So when my friend Bill Muir invited me to be a part of *The Lost Medallion,* a film where *kids* get to be the action heroes, I jumped at the chance.

Together we shaped and polished a film that follows two friends, Billy and Allie, on the adventure of a lifetime. Through it all, they learn a little about humility and faith and *a lot* about the limitless worth that God has placed on their lives.

Within these pages, you'll find that story. I've shared it with my own kids several times, and they love it. Really, that's all the introduction this book needs.

My hope is that your family loves it just as much as mine. And I pray that, through this adventure, your family will discover and rediscover the greatest treasure of all—the priceless value that God has placed on each and every one of your lives.

Enjoy the adventure!

Alex Kendrick

# Contents

# The Legend

*Aumakua Island, in the middle of the Pacific Ocean, 1819*

Fear drove his legs faster and faster as his bare feet pounded down the jungle path.

*Hurry! I must hurry,* he told himself, *or we will all die!*

Lungs burning, Faleaka pushed himself to still go faster as he raced toward the village. Sweat dripped down his golden brown skin and stung his eyes. At last, he caught sight of the village clearing and the statue of a man at its center. Around the statue's neck hung a golden medallion, glinting in the morning sunlight.

*The medallion!* he thought. *I must get to it! It's our only hope.*

As Faleaka ran toward the medallion, his thoughts went back to the day, years ago, when King Kieli had sacrificed

1

his own crown to make it. He had given up his crown to show his people that each of them was important, and that no one person was born greater than another.

Once the golden crown had been melted down and shaped into the medallion, the king had placed in its center a rare and beautiful blue stone. Because of the king's humility and great love for his people, the stone had taken on special powers, granting wishes—but only to the pure in heart.

Over the years, Faleaka had watched King Kieli use the powerful medallion to help his people. He had saved them from starvation by using it to grow crops during a terrible drought. He had used it to turn away terrible storms. And he had used it to defeat the invading armies of the evil warlord Cobra.

*But will it save us now?* Faleaka worried.

Reaching the statue, Faleaka snatched up the medallion. Gripping it tightly, he spun around and raced back toward the beach, where the king waited for him.

Along the path, Faleaka dodged fleeing villagers. Parents ran with small children. Warriors stopped to help the older and weaker. All of them desperate to escape the coming disaster. Faleaka also saw Huko, the king's own son, and his best friend, Anui, running—their eyes large with fear.

Seeing the frightened children, Faleaka forced himself to run even faster. Reaching the beach, he saw King Kieli standing at what had been the water's edge just moments ago—before the water had all been sucked away. The king's usually kind face was lined with worry as he stared up at the massive tidal wave roaring toward him—a hundred feet high and moving very fast.

*Too late, too late!* Faleaka worried. *I'll never make it in time.*

At just that moment, King Kieli looked behind him, his eyes searching for Faleaka. Seeing his trusted advisor and friend running toward him, Kieli shouted, "Hurry, Faleaka! The wave is almost upon us!"

Faleaka had no breath to answer his king. Instead, he focused on putting one foot in front of the other.

Kieli took a deep breath and turned back to face the wave that now blotted out the sun.

*I am not afraid to die,* he thought, *but my son, my people . . . I have failed them.*

Drops of water wet his face, and the strong, sharp smells of salt and fish filled his nose as the wall of water raged toward him. Kieli bowed his head, preparing for the end. But as he did so, Faleaka ran up and dropped the medallion over his head before falling to the sand in fear and exhaustion.

King Kieli then looked up to face the wave and, raising his hands high in the air, he shouted, "I command this wave to disappear!"

The medallion's stone began to glow with an unearthly blue light. Kieli and Faleaka watched in amazement as the wave froze briefly in midair before gently spilling itself back into the ocean. A frothy, two-foot-wave washed over them and then returned to the ocean with a gurgle.

Smiling with relief, Kieli turned and helped Faleaka to his feet. Together, they walked back to their small village of twenty huts. As the king entered the clearing, he was quickly surrounded by cheering villagers. The medallion had protected them once again.

Kieli made his way to the statue and carefully hung the medallion back in its place. The village and its people were safe. But by nightfall that would no longer be true.

★ ★ ★

*Later that same morning . . .*

The sun rose higher in the eastern sky, shining brightly over beautiful Aumakua Island. Lazy, tropical breezes drifted across the village, carrying scents of ripening pineapples and mangos from the surrounding jungle. Waterfalls splashed happily in the distance, giving music to the island paradise.

The village center was now deserted. With the danger past, the villagers had gone back to their everyday lives. While the grown-ups worked, the children swam in the cool, clear waters below a gentle waterfall. All was peaceful.

In the heart of the village, a bright red, island bird fluttered down and landed on the statue's shoulder. Tucking in its wings, it stood tall and proud, as if guarding the medallion—but only for a moment. An instant later, a small hand shooed it away.

"Stupid bird," said a young voice. "I am not interested in you."

The hand and the voice belonged to six-year-old Huko, the tall, wiry son of King Kieli. With dark, curly hair and brown eyes, he looked like a much younger version of his father—except that the kindness of King Kieli's face had already been replaced by pride and arrogance in Huko's. At this particular moment, Huko's face was filled with determination as he jumped again and again, trying to reach the medallion.

Throwing up his hands in frustration, Huko looked at his best friend, Anui, and said, "I need something to stand on."

Anui, who was also six, was a cheerful, round-faced boy. Plump and good-natured, he was always eager to follow Huko in his adventures—especially if they involved food. The two had been friends since they were toddlers and could usually be found together.

"Maybe you should just leave it alone," Anui suggested. He didn't want to get into trouble.

"Why should I?" Huko said, practicing his kingly voice. "When I am king, the medallion will be mine. I have a right to wear it."

"But won't you get into trouble?" Anui worried.

"When the people see it on me, they will bow and respect me, just as they do my father," Huko insisted.

"But . . ."

"Stop arguing, Anui," Huko shouted at him. "Help me think of a way to reach it."

"You could stand on my back," Anui offered.

"Good idea!"

Anui got down on all fours, his dark hair swinging forward over his face and hiding his brown eyes so that it was impossible for him to watch his friend's progress. Huko carefully climbed onto Anui's back. Steadying himself against the side of the statue, he slowly raised himself up to his full height.

"Hang on, I think I can reach it now," Huko said, glancing around to make sure no one was watching. Seeing no one, he quickly reached up, snatched the medallion from around the statue's neck, and jumped down. Clutching the treasure tightly to his thin chest, Huko sped off through the jungle to find a spot where he could enjoy his prize in secret. Anui puffed along behind him.

The boys raced through the jungle until they reached the path that led down to the beach. There, Huko slowed his pace, giving Anui a chance to catch up. But as he waited for Anui, Huko heard a rustling in the brush like footsteps.

"Hurry, Anui!" he hissed, keeping his voice low. "Someone is coming."

In spite of his earlier brave words, Huko was not eager to be caught with the medallion. Grabbing Anui's arm, Huko pulled him down the path and toward the beach.

"Come on! Come on!" Huko urged. "One of the grown-ups must have seen us."

The boys ran as fast as they could, but the sounds of someone behind them seemed to get closer. When they reached the white sand of the beach, the boys stopped to catch their breath.

"We are going to be in so much trouble," Anui moaned, as the rustling noises grew even louder.

Panicking, Huko began to stammer, "I . . . I am sorry. . . . I-I did not mean . . ."

With one last, loud crash, their pursuer burst out of the bushes and stared at them accusingly. Breathing a huge sigh of relief, the boys laughed as they saw that their pursuer was only a small, brown monkey, chattering and scolding them wildly. No one had been chasing them after all.

Still grinning, the boys ran down the sandy beach to

splash in the waves. Even though this was just an ordinary day, Huko wore the bright blue sash that showed him to be the future king—he liked to remind the villagers that he was royalty.

Huko and Anui played along the beach until they were both tired. Plopping down on the sand to rest, they shared made-up tales in which they were brave warriors fighting and defeating their deadly enemy Cobra. When at last they stood and turned back toward home, Huko put his arm around Anui's shoulders.

"You're the best friend a future king could ever have."

But as Huko looked down at his friend, his eyes fell upon the medallion hanging around his neck, and his heart almost stopped.

"Anui!" he shouted, pulling the medallion up for a closer look.

"What's wrong?" Anui asked curiously.

"The stone!"

Anui looked over at his friend and instantly saw the trouble. *The stone was gone!*

The boys stared at each other, the horrible truth sinking in. Without the stone, the medallion was powerless—and there was nothing to stop Cobra from invading their village. If they didn't find the stone, their stories of made-up battles would soon be very real.

The boys turned in circles, looking all around them. Dropping to their knees, they crawled along the path, pushing aside leaves and twigs to search the ground beneath. Then they combed the beach for what seemed like hours. Finally giving up, the boys realized they needed help and returned to the village. They found King Kieli carrying wood for an elderly woman.

As Huko approached his father, Kieli smiled and started to turn away, but his son's tear-stained face made him look back again. He walked over to Huko.

"What is wrong, my son?"

Unable to speak, Huko opened his hand and showed his father the medallion. The king's heart froze when he saw that the stone was missing. Dropping the wood, he knelt and asked, "Where did you take the medallion?"

"All over," Huko sniffed, hanging his head in shame.

"*Where*, Huko? Tell me where you carried the medallion!"

Huko pointed toward the path.

"Did you stay on the path?" the king asked.

"Yes, but then we played on the beach."

"Could it have been lost in the water?" the king asked, alarmed.

"Maybe."

Kieli ran to the village center and called to his people. Hearing the fear in their king's voice, they quickly dropped everything and came running. The village elders, including Faleaka, gently pushed their way to the front to stand beside Kieli.

Kieli looked around at the circle of worried faces and told them the terrible news. "The stone has been lost. We must search everywhere the boys have played. Break into teams and start looking. It *has* to be around here somewhere!"

The villager's worst fears were confirmed. Without the

stone, they knew they could not defend themselves against the Cobra and his armies.

Half the villagers followed Huko down the forest path, while the others went with Anui to the beach. Soon, men, women, and children were crawling all along the ground, searching every inch for the missing stone.

But there was one man who did not search. Slipping away unnoticed, Cobra's spy hurried through the heavy underbrush until he found a long forgotten path. He followed it to the edge of a cliff where a large drum was hidden in the jungle weeds. Pulling out the drum, he pounded out a message—a message that would betray his own people.

★ ★ ★

*On Cobra Island . . .*

The drumbeats floated across the ocean and into the ears of an enemy warrior, standing lookout high on a cliff. The warrior listened carefully to the message and then ran down the path toward Cobra's fortress to deliver the news.

Soon, the warrior stood with his message outside the doors of Cobra's throne room. As the two guards pulled back the heavy, double doors, one of them whispered to him, "Whatever you do, don't look into his eyes. It will mean your death."

Shaken, the warrior nodded and stepped inside.

Cobra's fortress was cold and foreboding, both inside and out. Carved from lava stone, its black columns cast dark shadows across the massive throne room. Golden metal arches held burning candles, but their angry flames gave no warmth and little light.

At the end of the enormous room stood Cobra's throne itself, high upon a platform. The throne was shaped like a hooded cobra about to strike and covered in pure gold. Behind it, another golden snake appeared to slither up the wall. Beside the throne, on a golden table, sat a small bowl carved from animal bone. Inside it, a deadly poison.

Below the throne, a large square had been carved into the stone floor. A guard stood near a lever on the opposite wall. At Cobra's command, the guard would pull the lever, and the square would slide open, revealing the very heart of the island's volcano. The warriors called it the "Pit of Death," and Cobra used it to destroy those who did not please him.

The warrior bowed deeply before Cobra, who was sitting on his throne. Tall and powerfully built, Cobra's head was sleek and bald like that of snake. A bright red cobra tattoo coiled around his arm. But the thing Cobra was best known for—and most feared for—was the fang-like fingernails of his right hand. The nails of his thumb and forefinger had been sharpened to resemble fangs—they were the reason for the bowl of poison. Cobra kept them coated in it. When angered, he would use those fang-like nails to strike his victims in the neck like a snake, killing them instantly.

Surrounded by ruthless warriors, Cobra had great power and led his army with an iron fist. But there was one thing he wanted more than anything else—Aumakua Island. Yet, he had never been able to defeat King Kieli or the power of the medallion.

Keeping his eyes downcast, the warrior nervously delivered his message, saying, "My lord, the medallion's stone has been lost."

Cobra smiled wickedly. *Now the islanders are helpless,* he thought.

Rising to his feet, Cobra addressed his warriors, "The stone has been lost, and Aumakua Island is now ours!"

The warriors raised their fists in the air and shouted, "Cobra! Cobra!"

"Gather your weapons, and man the boats. Tonight, we attack!"

★ ★ ★

### The Invasion

Warriors poured into dozens of sleek canoes, each with a single tall mast and a black sail bearing a bright red cobra. Armed with bows and arrows, spears, and machetes, they sailed soundlessly across the ocean and toward Aumakua Island. With the stone missing, the warriors knew that victory would be theirs. They also knew that failure was not an option, for Cobra destroyed those who failed him.

Unaware of the approaching danger, the villagers continued their frantic search for the stone until the sun sank into the ocean. Then they drifted one-by-one back to the village where they ate their evening meal in near silence.

As the villagers slept, Cobra's warriors glided to the shore, in their canoes, just as the sun was beginning to rise. Spilling out, they gathered quickly around their leader.

Keeping his voice low, Cobra hissed, "Attack! And this time, do not fail me."

Cobra's warriors charged forward, silently swarming the paths that took them to the village.

In the village, the mood was somber. Few had slept and most only picked at their morning meal. Suddenly, one of the men who had been standing lookout burst into the village clearing.

"Run!" he shouted. "They're coming!"

But before anyone could move, a loud *THWACK!* split the air as a deadly arrow pierced the man's back. His startled cry was brief as he clutched the shaft sticking out of his chest before falling to the ground.

Terrified screams filled the air as women snatched up their children and tried to escape. Men rushed to grab weapons to fight off the brutal attack, but their efforts were too late. Most were captured before they even reached their huts.

Huko and Anui had been walking toward their huts when the attack began. Anui's mother had grabbed them both, dragging them deep into the jungle to hide.

King Kieli, who had been in his hut praying to the One who gave the medallion its power, rushed outside as soon as he heard the screams. Spotting a villager about to stab one of Cobra's warriors, he ran over and grabbed the man's arm.

"No!" the king shouted. "We will not return evil with evil!"

Kieli then hurried to the village center and the statue. He grabbed up the medallion—even though it was powerless without the stone—and held it tightly in his hand. His presence brought the battle to a halt.

Standing defiantly, Kieli held his head high as Cobra stepped toward him. The two men eyed one another, each looking for the other's weakness. Cobra was the first to look away. Glancing at the statue, he saw that the medallion was missing.

While Cobra's head was turned, Kieli pulled the medallion from behind his back as though it were a weapon and raised it high for all to see. Cobra's men stepped back in fear, and one warrior ran away from the village, a mistake that would later cost him his life.

Cobra's eyes locked onto the prize he had sought for so long. With lightning speed he struck, moving so fast that even the king was taken by surprise, as the medallion was snatched from his grasp.

But Cobra didn't keep it long, as Faleaka tackled him and sent the medallion skipping across the grass.

While the two men fought, Kieli grabbed up the medallion and ran into the jungle, darting around trees and through the brush. His eyes searched everywhere for a place to hide the medallion—somewhere that Cobra would never find it.

Meanwhile, Faleaka fought desperately, trying to give the king time to escape. He knew that Kieli was not running in fear, but rather to protect the medallion. But Cobra was stronger. He broke free and slashed Faleaka's face, sending him to his knees. Cobra followed that with a vicious blow to the back of his head, and Faleaka dropped to the ground, unconscious. Grabbing a machete from one of his warriors, Cobra disappeared into the jungle after Kieli.

Kieli heard Cobra's footsteps coming closer. Stronger and much swifter, Cobra smashed through the brush until he spotted Kieli crossing a small clearing.

Cobra took aim and hurled his machete, but Kieli ducked and it flew over his head, sticking in a nearby tree. Fearing another attack, Kieli dove into the under-brush, crawling behind a boulder that was strangely shaped like a man. Cobra did not see where Kieli had gone and ran past him.

Knowing he was out of time, Kieli quickly dug a hole in the soft earth with his hands. When it was deep enough, he ripped off his royal sash and wrapped the medallion inside the blue cloth. Clutching the medallion to him for the brief-est of seconds, he begged the Great King to protect the medallion and his people. He then placed the bundle in the hole and filled in the dirt. Placing a large stone on top, he covered it all with leaves and grass so that the placed looked as if it had never been undisturbed.

Slipping out of his hiding spot, the king quietly made his way toward an opening in the dense trees. He hadn't gone far when Cobra suddenly stepped out in front of him. With one swift, hard blow, he knocked Kieli to the ground.

"Where is it?" Cobra demanded, towering over the fallen man.

"Safe," the king said, "where you will never find it!"

Spitting with anger, Cobra raised his hand and then struck. The poisoned fangs of his fingers sank deep into King Kieli's neck, stopping his heart instantly. The good king was dead.

## Chapter 1

# The Dig Site

**Aumakua Island, Present Day**

The tires of a battered, blue dirt bike skidded to a stop on the dusty road. A worn boot lowered the kickstand, and thirteen-year-old Billy Stone hopped off. Dressed in faded cargo pants, a short-sleeved shirt, and a khaki vest covered in pockets, his dark hair was damp with sweat. Eyes shining with a mixture of excitement and fear of discovery, he scanned the razor wire-topped fence that surrounded the dig site.

Reaching into his worn leather pack, Billy pulled out a ring of thin, metal lock picks. Keeping an eye out for guards, he selected a pick and set to work on the padlock securing the main gate.

Inside the fence, a tired, dust-covered worker rounded the corner, heading for the gate. Billy flattened himself to the ground, holding his breath as the worker approached, ready to jump up and make a run for it, if necessary. But the man, completely unaware of Billy's presence, walked past without even seeing him.

Breathing a sigh of relief, Billy went back to work on the lock. Having done this many times before, the lock soon popped open with a soft *click!* Billy tucked the picks back into his pack and slipped inside the gate, pulling it closed behind him.

Bent low, Billy darted from one hiding place to another, crouching behind trees and pieces of equipment. Slowly, he made his way to a large tent that served as the dig site's headquarters. Seeing no one around, Billy dropped and quickly rolled under the bottom of one of the tent walls.

Inside, technicians worked at tables covered with artifacts, laptops, and soil testers. One wall was completely covered with maps, each dotted with marking pins and scribbled notes. The other walls were lined with either filing cabinets or tables loaded with artifacts and digging tools. Keeping low under the tables, Billy edged his way toward the tools. Reaching up, he snatched a small kit from one of the tables. Now all he had to do was keep quiet and roll back under the edge of the tent to escape.

But at that moment, one of the men sprayed a recent find with compressed air, sending a cloud of dust into the air and up Billy's nose. Pinching his nose shut, Billy covered his mouth and tried to stifle the sneeze. Praying no one would notice, he jerked up the bottom of the tent and rolled under. The instant he was outside, the sneeze exploded out, startling the workers inside the tent.

But, glancing around, they saw no one. Shrugging, they returned to their work.

Billy took cover behind a nearby bush. Pausing to get his bearings, he spotted a weathered-looking man, obviously the dig's boss, studying a map with one of the workers. Billy knew he couldn't let the boss see him, or he'd be in real trouble.

Sprinting off in the opposite direction, Billy ran until he came to a large hole about a hundred feet square and three feet deep. Dropping down into it, he carefully spread out his tools—much like a surgeon—and went to work.

First choosing a small, sharp-pointed trowel, Billy began digging into the soft dirt along the wall of the hole. He hadn't been working long, when his trowel scraped something hard. Gently loosening the dirt around it, he pulled the object from the earth. Picking up a soft brush, he carefully dusted away layers of  dirt, revealing the end of a two-hundred-year-old fishing spear. As Billy studied his find, a shadow fell over him.

"I want you out of here," the boss said angrily. "I want you off this site right now!"

Billy stood up and faced the man. "Let me help you," he pleaded.

"You can't help," the boss said with hint of sadness in his voice. "You don't belong here."

"But I'm an archeologist!" Billy insisted.

"You're thirteen, and I don't have time to worry about you."

"Please!" he begged. "I . . . I can clean tools, take notes, get coffee . . . dig holes."

The boss shook his head, "You're too young for this kind of work."

"You never used to say that," Billy accused. "Come on, I'll do *anything* you need."

"Promise?"

"Yeah, I promise," Billy said, his hopes beginning to rise.

"Go home."

Billy's heart sank. "But . . . Dad . . ."

"Dad" was forty-six-year-old Dr. Michael Stone. Once a world-famous archeologist, Dr. Stone was now something of a joke in the archaeological world. His quest to find the lost royal medallion—a medallion that many archaeologists didn't even believe existed—had become an obsession, ruining first his career and then his family. His once-handsome face was now weathered and lined, his brown hair streaked with gray. Staring down at his rebellious son, he scowled.

"But, Dad . . . there's no one there," Billy finished painfully.

Taking Billy by the arm, Dr. Stone led him back to the main gate. "Go home, Billy," he insisted, shoving him outside and locking the gate before walking away.

Billy stared after his father before turning back toward his bike. Kicking a rock, he sent it skipping across the dirt road. The last thing he wanted was to go home.

When Billy's mom, Kale'a, had been alive, home had been a wonderful place to go back to. The house had always been filled with music and singing and delicious smells coming from the oven. But with his mother gone, "home" was just an empty house full of painful memories.

As Billy walked, head down, he almost ran into two men, who were stapling papers to the dig site's fence. Billy recognized them as Cobb's thugs.

Cobb was the most powerful—and the most evil—man on Aumakua Island. Though he pretended to be a respectable businessman, in reality, he was nothing more than a thug himself. A thug with a lot of money—he practically owned the entire island. Few people were willing to cross him.

One of Cobb's thugs was named Kalani. He was thin with dark, wavy hair that hugged his scalp and framed shifty eyes. He was known for being extremely intelligent—unlike his partner, Makala.

Makala was huge and strong with a patchy, coarse beard. He was Kalani's opposite in every way . . . except cruelty. Both men bore the blood-red tattoos of a cobra on their right arms, marking them as Cobb's men.

Kalani looked down at Billy. "You know," he said, his voice turning sickly sweet, "we could use an archaeologist like you on our team. Cobb appreciates your talents, while certain others . . ." he said, jerking his head back toward the dig site and Billy's father, "do not."

Billy ignored the remark, his eyes scanning the papers they had stapled up. Seeing the word "foreclosure" in large, black letters, Billy was furious. Lunging past Makala, he ripped the papers off the fence.

Makala grabbed Billy's arms and held him. "Are you kidding me?" he said, giving Billy a rough shake. "Gimme those," he barked, snatching the papers back. Then shoving Billy toward his bike, he shouted, "Get lost, you little brat!"

Billy threw the men a disgusted look, then jumped on his bike and angrily cranked the engine. Zooming off through the jungle-like terrain, he splashed through streams and jumped small hills. His tires squealed loudly as he hit the paved road and headed for town.

Kalani and Makala finished stapling up the notices and then climbed into the front of a sleek, black sedan.

"What do you think, Mr. Cobb?" Makala asked, as they both turned to face the man sitting in the shadows of the back seat.

Cobb looked at them coolly. He was heavily muscled with sleek, black hair that he wore pulled into a low ponytail. Everything about him—from his cold, dark eyes to his expensive black suit—suggested cruelty. It was something he had inherited from his ancestor—Cobra.

Cobb answered, "Our families have been searching for the medallion for generations. This kid is on to something. Keep an eye on him."

"Not to worry," Kalani assured him, "we come from a long line of trackers."

# Chapter 2

# Two Friends, Two Spies

Billy rode his dirt bike through town. He had fixed up the bike himself over the winter, and it was his pride and joy. But today, not even his bike could lift his anger . . . or his sadness.

He rode through the town, glaring at the signs—Cobb's Grocery, Cobb's Gas Station, Cobb's Hardware. Everything in the town belonged to "Cobb Enterprises, Inc." It had been years since the buildings had received a fresh coat of paint, the roads were pitted with holes, and everything was overrun with weeds. Everywhere Billy looked, people trudged along the sidewalks like broken slaves, living a life without hope.

Speeding through the center of town, Billy passed the cracked and neglected stone statue of a man who had once been honored, his importance forgotten over the years.

The statue had been found on one of his father's archaeological digs and brought here to the center of town. That had been an exciting time. But it had also been long ago, before everything had gone wrong.

Billy left the town behind and headed down a well-worn, dirt path through the jungle until he reached a thirty-foot cliff. A small waterfall tumbled over its edge, spilling into a crystal clear pool. Billy parked his bike and headed toward the cliff's edge. Determination replaced anger as he peered over, watching the water drop off into the pool below.

Billy loved this place; its wildness was far better than the crumbling concrete of town. Heading over to a nearby banana tree, he carefully examined several leaves before finally plucking one and returning to the edge of the falls.

Billy stood for a moment, eyes down and face calm, as he concentrated. Then, taking a deep breath and  firing up his courage, he sprinted to the edge and . . . jumped, flinging the giant banana leaf over his head like a parachute. But the leaf fluttered uselessly, and he dropped like a stone. A strangled cry escaped his lips just before he plunged into the icy water.

★ ★ ★

Sitting on a rock below the falls, thirteen-year-old Allie had been buried in her book—*Finding Values with Simple Equations*—until she heard Billy's cry. Looking up, she watched her friend belly-flop painfully into the water with a loud smack, before bobbing back to the surface.

"Ouch!" she winced, shaking her head. Smart and energetic, Allie was a tomboy in overalls who preferred reading books to almost anything else. She was also Billy's best friend.

As Billy paddled toward her, Allie raised an eyebrow and peered at him with blue-green eyes. Pushing dark blonde hair behind her ears, she wrinkled her freckled nose at him. "You know . . . you weren't created to fly. At least not like that," she said, laughing.

Billy shook the water from his head and crawled ashore, gasping for breath.

"From that height, at your weight," Allie calculated, "you would need *at least* four-and-a-half times more surface area for your parachute."

"Where'd you get that idea?" he asked, collapsing next to her on the ground.

"It's amazing what you can learn from a book," she said. "You should open one sometime."

"What I'm looking for can't be found in a book."

"You might be surprised," Allie teased. Then, turning serious, she asked, "Did you get kicked out again?"

"Yeah," Billy sighed. "My dad's never gonna let me join him."

"Well, did you find anything interesting *before* you got kicked out?"

Billy frowned and dug a hole in the sand. "Nah, not really . . ." Then, his voice changed, as a glimmer of hope crept in, ". . . not yet anyway. But someday, the entire world will be changed when I find the medallion."

"How's that?" Allie asked.

"Mom really wanted Dad to find that medallion. But searching for it took over my dad's whole life. Don't you see? If I found the medallion, it would change everything. I could save the dig site from Cobb."

*And then my dad would have to respect me,* Billy thought to himself.

Allie sighed. "It's too bad your parents never found the medallion. They spent so much time looking for it. People around here might have given your mom the respect she deserved as a descendant of King Kieli and King Huko."

"Yeah," Billy agreed. "Mom believed that if Dad found the medallion *and* the stone, it would restore her family's reputation—everyone blames our family because Huko lost the stone. And the medallion would give the people hope. Mom even thought that because she was a direct descendant of the king that she might be able to use the medallion to heal the island. She's gone now, but . . . I'm a descendant too. Maybe I could use it to get rid of Cobb."

Allie closed her book and stuffed it into her book bag. "Hey, what's at the site where your dad's working now, anyway?"

Allie knew that over the years, Billy's dad had worked at dig sites all over Aumakua Island, as well as neighboring Cobra Island.

"He thinks he's found Faleaka's hut."

"Really? How does he know it was Faleaka's hut?"

"He found Faleaka's staff," Billy said.

"So Faleaka really did survive Cobra's attack?"

"Yeah, but Dad thinks Faleaka felt guilty," Billy explained. "As the king's closest friend and advisor, it was his job to protect the king. When he failed, Dad thinks Faleaka was too ashamed to return to the village. So he built this hut away from everyone and lived there in hiding until he died."

"That's so sad," Allie said, standing up and brushing the dirt from her overalls. "Well, it's getting late. I guess I'd better get back."

Billy stood up with her. "Someday I *am* going to find that medallion."

"Someday, *we'll* find the medallion," Allie insisted.

Billy smiled, and the two friends began to make their way through the jungle and back to Billy's bike.

★ ★ ★

As Billie and Allie made their way back to the bike, Cobb's thugs stepped out from their hiding place in the trees. They had clearly been spying on the two friends.

"And so the spider sees the fly," said Kalani cryptically.

Makala stared at him blankly and shook his head. *Why can't he just talk normal?* he wondered for the thousandth time.

★ ★ ★

Billy and Allie climbed back up to the top of the falls where Billy had parked his dirt bike. Getting on behind him, Allie buckled on her helmet before wrapping her arms tightly around Billy's waist for the ride home. As they took off, neither of them noticed the black jeep that pulled out behind them and began following them at a distance.

A short ride later, Billy pulled up in front of a neglected-looking building. The battered sign out front read "Aumakua Orphanage." Allie hopped off the bike just as the black jeep coasted to a stop behind a broken-down truck on the side of the road.

"See ya tomorrow," she said, handing Billy her helmet and turning toward the front door. Halfway there, she remembered something and turned back.

"Hey, I almost forgot," she said, digging into her book bag and pulling out an old, weather-beaten journal. "I found this at a used bookstore. It's some kind of antiquarian journal about our island," she said.

"A *what* journal?" Billy asked.

"An *old* journal. You should give it a read," she said, handing it to him. "You might find something interesting."

Allie stuffed her hands in pockets and turned again to go. "See ya," she called.

"Hey, Allie! When are you gonna let me see inside that place?" Billy asked, his hopes rising.

"When there's something worth seeing," she called back.

The orphanage was the only thing Allie wouldn't talk to Billy about. She hid the pain of living there from everyone. She even tried to hide it from herself by staying buried in her books.

Billy tucked the journal in his pack and sped off. Since Allie was already headed inside, she didn't see the black jeep pull out and follow Billy.

## Chapter 3

# Lost Hope

Stepping inside the orphanage, Allie tried to ignore the ugly, green walls and scuffed brown floors. She walked up to a battered, wooden receptionist's desk and looked at the woman seated there hopefully.

"Did my mom call today?" she asked.

"You have asked me that question every day since you got here," the woman snapped, not even bothering to look up from her paperwork. "The answer's still the same. No. The answer will always be . . . no."

Allie's heart sank. *I should just face the truth,* she thought. *My mother doesn't want me . . . nobody wants me.*

Then, giving herself a little shake, she squared her shoulders. Her face set with determination, she headed up the worn staircase—where she met the two worst bullies in the orphanage.

Allie tried to be pleasant. "Hey, how was school today?" she asked.

The girls glared at her with open hatred.

"Better get busy, Allie," one of them sneered. "Head mistress won't like it if she finds out you stayed out all day without doing your chores."

"I finished my chores this morning," Allie snapped back, stomping up the stairs. "And don't worry, you won't be seeing me around here much longer."

But the girls just snickered and kept walking.

Allie trudged up to the third floor. *That was stupid, Allie,* she scolded herself. *Why do I even bother trying to be nice to those girls? I hate this place!*

Allie argued with herself all the way down the hall until she reached her small, dingy room at the far end. It was difficult to tell what color the walls were supposed to be—most of the paint had faded away over the years. The bare, tile floors were a cold, mottled grey. But Allie had tried to make the best of it. Her bed, though rickety and covered with an old tattered quilt, was kept neatly made. Her windowsill was filled with pretty shells and rocks she'd collected in her explorations with Billy. The only other furniture in the room was a hard, wooden chair and a shabby chest that held her few clothes.

But this time, when Allie entered her room, she found her quilt wadded up in the floor and her few clothes thrown around the room—all of them tracked with mud. Allie threw her bag down furiously, as the meaning of the other girl's words sank in.

She stood staring at the mess until she remembered— *the bathroom!* It had been her day to clean the bathroom.

Allie raced out of the room and down the hall. Slumping against the bathroom wall, she saw that it, too, was tracked and smeared with mud.

Furious, Allie wanted to chase down those girls and tear their hair out, but she knew she had to get the mess cleaned up before bed check or she'd be in deep trouble. It took her hours to clean everything. Rinsing out the last of her clothes in the sink late that night, tears of frustration ran down Allie's cheeks.

After spreading her clothes out to dry on the now clean floor, an exhausted Allie dropped onto her small bed, the springs squeaking in protest. And as she did each night, she pulled out a worn and creased picture of her mother. Gazing at it, she tried to remember the good times they'd had together—and to forget the bad.

The only thing Allie knew for certain was that she could not stand another day in this place. She *had* to get away. Making up her mind, Allie got down on her knees and pulled out her suitcase. Enough was enough.

★ ★ ★

It was late afternoon when Billy reached home and parked his bike in front of their yellow, stucco house. Jogging around to the back, he found his dad sitting on the porch, head buried in his hands.

Billy stopped. "Dad, you okay?" he asked in a worried voice.

Shaking his head, Dr. Stone looked up at Billy sadly.

"It's over," he said, his voice dead.

"What's over?" Billy asked.

"Cobb shut me down," Dr. Stone said, running his hand through his hair.

"But . . . you owe the bank, not him!" Billy argued.

"Cobb *is* the bank, Billy," Dr. Stone told him. "He owns everything on this island, including the dig site now. I give up."

"No, Dad! You can't give up! *We* can't give up, Dad! If we give up, Cobb will find the medallion and win."

"The medallion?" Dr. Stone shouted bitterly. "I've lost everything! And for what? Some nonexistent medallion?"

Billy moved closer to his father, a pleading expression on his face. "You know Mom would tell you that it exists! You *know* she'd want you to keep looking," he insisted.

"Even she would have to admit that it's useless to go on now, Billy. I'm a failure. A thousand holes, and what do I have to show for it? Nothing! I've lost everything, looking for some worthless, nonexistent piece of stone."

"But it does exist, Dad. I can *feel* it. It's in the ground somewhere. I know it is," Billy insisted.

Dr. Stone looked straight into Billy's eyes, his voice empty and cold, and said, "Everything that has ever meant anything to me is buried in the ground."

The words hit Billy like a fist. Turning away from his dad, he stormed inside the house and up to his room.

Dr. Stone didn't even notice that Billy had left. He hadn't meant to hurt him. He was just lost in his own misery and didn't see how deeply his words had wounded his only son.

★ ★ ★

In his room, Billy threw his pack on the floor and plopped down at his desk. Seeing a picture of himself smiling happily with his parents, Billy thought back to the times he used to spend with his dad . . . the good times. Billy knew that his father had once gone on digs all over the world. But then, years ago, he had come to Aumakua Island to investigate the legend of the Lost Medallion. And it was here, that he had met Kale'a, Billy's mom. She'd been an historian, an expert on the legends of Aumakua and Cobra Islands. And as a descendant of the great King Kieli himself, she had convinced the world-renowned Dr. Stone that the legend of the medallion and its stone was real. Michael had given up his other digs and concentrated on the medallion. And as they'd searched together for the medallion, they'd also fallen in love and married.

When Billy came along, he had helped his parents, especially his dad. Together, they had hiked through the jungles, mapped out dig sites, and dug deep into the earth, looking for the legendary medallion. It had only been a couple of years ago that they had explored Cobra's Island, mapping out its maze of underground caves. And then, they had found Faleaka's hut. His father had even allowed Billy to take Faleaka's staff home with him. Billy remembered helping his dad clean the intricately carved hawk at the top of the staff. Though its wings had been broken off long ago, it was still magnificent and strong. *That* had been a wonderful day.

*That* had also been the day that everything changed. That was the day they had gotten the news. The news that Billy's mom wasn't just tired, she was dying of cancer. And that was the day that his dad had started to change.

Looking around his room, Billy saw the quilt his mother had made him, laying across his bed. He saw the maps of the islands, dotted with pins marking all the places he and his dad had explored. Scattered everywhere were old fishing spears, tools, and arrows they had unearthed together. His mother's hand-drawn sketches of King Kieli and Cobra lay on his desk.

*I miss the way things used to be,* he thought.

Digging through his desk, Billy pulled out a small, blackened stone. Turning it over in his fingers, he remembered the day his mother had given it to him. She had been so weak, she could no longer get out of bed. Her beautiful face was lined and her once shining black hair had dulled. But her eyes had still been warm and filled with love as Billy sat next to her on the bed.

"I want you to have this," she said, showing him the stone. "It's been in my family for a long time. I know it doesn't look like much, but there's something very special about it. It is said that King Huko believed this was *the* stone . . . the stone from the medallion. Legend says he found it after searching for years—though, without the medallion, there's no way to know if it is the real stone. The legend also says that one day the true king will return to Aumakua Island with the medallion and free his people."

Kale'a smiled weakly and placed the stone in Billy's hand. Then, picking up the worn Bible that never left her side these days, she added, "Just as our Great King will return one day and free us from this world." Patting his arm, she whispered, "I love you, honey," she whispered before drifting off to sleep.

Looking at the stone now, Billy missed his mom so badly it hurt. When she'd gotten sick, his dad had become completely obsessed with finding the medallion, believing that if he could somehow find it, then he could cure his wife. And when she died, the obsession had only grown stronger, so that there was little room in his life for his son. Billy had lost not only his mom, but his dad as well.

Sighing, Billy noticed that the sun was beginning to set and his room was growing dark. Putting down the stone, he snapped on a lamp and picked up his pack. Searching through it, he pulled out firecrackers, a compact fishing pole, a small shovel and pick axe, his ring of lock picks, a flashlight, binoculars, and a slingshot before finally finding what he was looking for—the journal Allie had given him.

Sitting back down at his desk, he opened the journal. The pages were brown and brittle with age. Scanning the pages filled with poetry and drawings, Billy quickly became bored. He set the journal aside and picked up the stone again, along with two others and began juggling them. It was something he often did when he needed to think. Getting to his feet, he walked over the maps of Aumakua Island and began to study them closely, his thoughts churning.

★ ★ ★

Billy's actions did not go unnoticed. Outside, Cobb's thugs were perched on the sturdy limbs of a large tree, giving them a direct line of sight into Billy's room.

Makala leaned against the wide trunk, watching Billy juggle through his binoculars. "The kid's pretty good," he admitted.

"Cobb thinks he's onto something," Kalani said, adjusting his headphones. They were hooked up to a sophisticated, parabolic listening device, which he kept pointed at Billy's room.

Makala put down his binoculars and said, "He's just standing around juggling. How much longer do we have to stay here?"

Kalani smiled darkly as he said, "We sleep not 'til this mission be complete."

Something important was about to happen. Kalani could feel it, and he was prepared to do whatever it took to help his boss find the medallion—knowing that his reward would be great. Of course, he also knew that if he failed Cobb, his punishment would be terrible. Kalani shuddered and then fixed his attention on Billy once more.

stool in front of his dad's favorite chair. *They're in the living room!* Billy thought, starting to panic.

Hands shaking, Billy raised the staff high above his head as the footsteps moved up the stairs toward him. When the intruder reached the fifth step from the landing, it creaked loudly. The sound brought a wry smile to Billy's face—that step was the closest thing to a burglar alarm they had.

As the footsteps came still closer, Billy saw a shadow creeping up the stairwell wall. He held the staff high, preparing to strike. As the intruder stepped onto the landing, Billy took a deep breath and swung as hard as he could.

## Chapter 5

# The Unexpected Clue

There was a loud scream followed by a terrific thud as the intruder ducked and the staff bounced off the wall.

"What are you doing?" Allie screamed.

"I was going to ask you that!" Billy yelled back.

★ ★ ★

Outside in the yard, Makala and Kalani had almost reached the back door when Kalani dropped to his knees, writhing in pain—Allie's shriek, amplified through the listening device, had exploded in his ears.

Makala, not understanding, reached down and yanked his partner to his feet. "This is no time for a break. Come on, get up," he whispered.

"Wait," Kalani said. "That girl's with him. Maybe they'll talk about what's in that old book."

"So what if they do?"

"We might learn something that will lead us to the medallion," Kalani snapped.

"And if we don't?"

"*Then* we go in and grab the kid. I'm tired of waiting for him to talk."

★ ★ ★

Inside the house, Allie leaned against the wall, trying to catch her breath and slow her pounding heart. She stared at Billy, stunned.

"What are you *doing*?" she managed to ask again.

"I thought you were an intruder. Why did you sneak in?" Billy asked as they headed into his room.

"I wasn't sneaking," she said defensively. "I knocked on the front door, But no one answered. I tried the handle, and it was unlocked, so I came in. I saw the light in your room . . . I didn't think you'd mind."

"No, but how'd you get out of the orphanage?" Billy asked. "I thought you weren't allowed out at night."

"I snuck out."

"Why?" Billy asked.

"I wanted to talk to you," Allie said her eyes filling with tears. "I've decided I'm gonna run away."

"What?" Billy asked in disbelief. "Why?"

"I wanna find my mom."

"But, Allie, you don't even know where she is," Billy reasoned.

"I know where she isn't—the orphanage!"

Billy leaned the staff back against the wall, trying to figure out something to say to his best friend.

Spotting the open journal on his desk, Allie picked it up and asked, "Read anything interesting?"

Billy shook his head. "No, I haven't really read it yet," he admitted

"Oh," Allie said, her disappointment clearly showing.

Suddenly Billy had an idea. "Listen," he said. "Promise me you won't run away, and we'll read it together."

Allie smiled and nodded.

Tossing a bunch of pillows on the floor, Billy and Allie settled down to look through the journal. Allie lay on her stomach, absentmindedly swinging her leg back and forth, her shoe dangling off her foot, while Billy paged through the journal.

"There's nothing here but a lot of mushy poetry that some girl wrote," he said with disgust, pushing the book toward Allie.

"There *has* to be something in here," Allie said, skimming through the carefully written words.

"I hope you're right, but I've flipped through half of it and haven't found anything about the medallion," Billy said.

Allie scanned the entries, reading bits and pieces, until she stopped and pointed to a page.

"Read this one . . . from June, 18, 1827. It's an entry by Mohea—she's the one who wrote this journal," she said, handing Billy the journal as she rolled over and gazed at the ceiling covered with glow-in-the-dark stars.

Billy started to read. "'His eyes were filled with the passion of waves on a summer day; his arms as strong as the mountains . . .' There's no way I'm reading this romantic stuff," Billy said, slapping the journal down on the floor.

Allie groaned, then rolled over and propped up on her elbows. Flipping through the journal again, she said, "Try this one."

"July 28, 1828," Billy read. "Rocks fell from the angry face of the mountains, filling our valley with sadness."

"Well?" Allie prompted.

"Well, what? It's just a bunch of gushy poetry."

"Don't you see it? 'Rocks fell . . .'?"

Billy thought for a moment. "Hey! She's talking about an earthquake!"

"Exactly!" Allie said, looking smug. "Now, this is where you say, 'I see the value of books now, Allie.'" Billy read on. "'What once was a short walk became a very long one.'" Billy looked puzzled.

"Well?" Allie said.

"Well, what?" Billy said again.

"The earthquake moved it," Allie said simply.

"The earthquake moved the medallion?"

"Not the medallion . . . the river!" she explained.

Billy stared at her blankly for a moment. Then suddenly, his eyes grew wide as the full meaning of what Allie had said hit him. Jumping up, they both headed for the map on the wall. Using her finger, Allie traced the river and examined the land around it.

"Here," she said, pointing to a bend in the land's topography.

"Yeah, I see it," Billy agreed. "With a little imagination, it could be an old riverbed."

Billy grabbed a marker off his desk and traced the path where the river's original course would have flowed toward the sea. When he finished, they grinned at each other.

"Dad's been looking on the wrong side of the river!" he exclaimed excitedly.

"Let's go tell him," Allie said.

"No," Billy stopped her, remembering his father's earlier words. "I have to find the medallion myself."

"Why?"

"Dad always chases me away from the digs. He says I only get in the way. If I find the medallion, he'll have to respect me," Billy said. *And maybe he'll even love me,* he thought to himself.

"Okay, but don't you dare go without me!" Allie warned. "If we're doing this without your dad, then we're doing it together.

★ ★ ★

Outside, the two thugs had climbed back into the tree. With the kids on the floor, Makala couldn't see anything through his binoculars and had fallen asleep against the tree trunk. Kalani, however, listened closely, straining to hear every word. As the kids excitedly discussed their plans to search for the medallion, Kalani smiled to himself.

*This is it,* he thought, *the information we've been waiting for!*

Reaching up, he whacked Makala across the back of the head. "Time to go, sleeping beauty, we've got a lead," he said.

Startled, Makala yelled . . . right into the listening device. Kalani shrieked and fell out of the tree, landing with a thud.

Makala snickered as he climbed down to help his partner.

**Chapter 6**

# The Hunt Js On

The next day found Billy and Allie deep in the jungle on another part of the island. Billy swept a battered-looking metal detector back and forth through the tall vegetation.

"Billy, why don't you just buy one of those things. I mean, look at it. It's half-broken," Allie said.

"Because they're more fun to make," Billy answered, concentrating on the soft beeping sound.

Every time the detector went off, he would stop and dig a hole while Allie peered over his shoulder. Thus far, they had found $1.73 in change, five very old bottle caps, three rusty nails, and half a dozen spoons. The sun was now high in the morning sky. Billy was getting frustrated, but he was determined not to quit until he'd found the medallion.

As they moved farther into the dense trees, the detector suddenly began beeping rapidly. Billy and Allie dropped to

43

their knees. Quickly pulling a small trowel out of his pack, Billy started digging. At first, he didn't find anything.

"Maybe you need to dig deeper," Allie suggested.

Billy nodded and kept digging. Finally, his shovel scraped against something metal. Grinning excitedly, Billy brushed away more of the dirt with his fingers. But his face fell when the object turned out to be another old spoon.

"I swear, if I find one more spoon . . ." Billy growled in frustration, flinging the spoon off into the jungle.

Allie rolled her eyes. "Well, you'll probably find that one again," she muttered to herself as Billy filled in the dirt and returned the trowel to his pack.

★ ★ ★

A hundred yards away, twelve men with metal detectors walked side-by-side, conducting their own search for the medallion, with Kalani and Makala leading the way.

★ ★ ★

Billy dug a map of the island out of his pack and studied it. "If Cobra chased Kieli this way, then he had to stop somewhere along here to bury the medallion," Billy said, pointing farther down the path they were on. "And he had to do it before Cobra caught up to him. Otherwise, Cobra would have seen where Kieli buried it."

"Maybe if we knew where the king was headed, we'd have a better idea of where to look," Allie said.

"That's just it . . . no one knows," Billy said. "Kieli couldn't tell anyone what he had in mind—not with the enemy all around him. But if the village was located where we think it was, he would have most likely run this way to escape Cobra."

Unknown to Billy and Allie, Cobb's men were now less than fifty yards away from them. When one of their metal detectors began beeping loudly, Billy and Allie jumped, startled by the noise. Billy carefully edged toward the sound. Pushing aside some leaves, he peered through the brush and spotted the men.

"Allie, it's Cobb's men!" he hissed.

"How do you know?" Allie whispered.

"Who else would it be?" Billy replied. "Cobb is the only one besides my dad and me trying to find the medallion."

At that moment, the men turned and started moving straight toward them. Billy pulled Allie down behind a large banyan tree.

"What are they doing here?" she whispered, frightened.

"I don't know. It doesn't make sense. We just decided to check this area last night. It's almost as if . . ."

". . . as if they were listening to every word we said," Allie whispered angrily.

As the men came even closer, the kids heard Kalani yell, "Keep looking, you buffoons! Cobb wants that medallion found or else!"

With the men now only about twenty feet away from their hiding place, another metal detector began screeching loudly. One of the men bent down, picking up the spoon Billy had thrown earlier. With a look of disgust, he flung it away, just as another of the men called out, "Hey! I think I've found something!"

Kalani, Makala, and the others ran off in the direction of the man's voice.

Billy watched until they were out of sight before saying, "Okay, let's go!"

He and Allie stood up from their hiding place.

Heading in the opposite direction of Cobb's men, Billy said, "We need to rethink this. The legend says the king died over there, and the village is that way, so which direction would he have gone?"

The two continued talking while they moved down the trail, occasionally glancing back to make sure Cobb's men had not returned. But soon they were so distracted by their own search that they didn't see Cobb's men coming up from the side.

"Get them!" Kalani yelled as they lunged after Billy and Allie.

## Chapter 7

# A Strange Wind

"Run!" Billy cried, when he saw Cobb's men coming after them.

Billy and Allie ducked down a side path with Kalani and Makala in close pursuit. As he ran, Billy spotted a tree ahead with a low-hanging branch. He grabbed Allie's hand and pulled her in that direction.

Cobb's thugs were only a few feet behind them. Reaching the tree, Billy grabbed the branch, pulling it with him as he and Allie ran past. Then, just as the thugs were about to catch up, he let go. The branch snapped back, hitting Kalani and Makala squarely in the chest and knocking them to the ground. Billy and Allie quickly darted off the path and out of sight—unknowingly following the same route that King Kieli had followed so many years before.

While Kalani and Makala picked themselves up, Billy spotted a hiding place amongst the roots of a giant banyan tree, near a strange-looking, man-shaped rock. He and Allie hid between the roots until they heard Cobb's men heading off in the opposite direction.

Peeking around the tree for any sign of Cobb's men, Allie's foot accidentally kicked the metal detector. Landing on a new spot, it began beeping loudly.

"Stop it! Make it stop!" Allie said in a horrified whisper as Billy dove for the machine, pushing it to a different spot so that the beeping stopped. When Makala and Kalani did not appear, Billy picked up the detector and waved it over the ground. Once again it beeped loudly. Tossing the detector to the side, Billy pulled the trowel out of his pack.

A large stone sat in the middle of the spot where the detector had beeped. Billy moved it to the side and started digging.

As he dug, a strange wind blew over them, ruffling their hair and rustling the leaves. Billy looked at Allie, eyes wide, then began digging even faster. Allie watched, nervously gnawing a thumbnail. Hearing a soft, metallic *clink!*, Billy dropped the trowel and used his hands to dig.

Gently brushing away the dirt, Billy discovered a bundle of tattered blue cloth. Lifting it up, he looked at it closely.

"It's King Kieli's emblem," Billy whispered, his voiced filled with awe.

Carefully unwrapping the cloth, Billy hardly dared to breathe as a golden edge appeared. Pulling away the rest of the cloth, the royal medallion winked at him in the sunlight, almost as clean and shiny as the day it had been buried.

"We found it!" Billy whispered. "We found it."

Billy handed the medallion to Allie so that she could get a better look.

"Just wait 'til my dad sees this!" Billy said, taking the medallion back.

A shadow fell over him and a voice behind them said, "A serendipitous day, is it not?"

Billy whirled around to see Kalani.

"You a good arco-lala-gist," Makala said.

Kalani moved closer. "I believe you have what is ours," he said menacingly, holding out his hand. "May we give you a ride into town?"

Stuffing the medallion in his pack, Billy grabbed Allie's arm and took off, shouting, "Come on, Allie!"

"Seize them!" shouted Kalani.

"Get back here!" ordered Makala.

Once again, Billy and Allie were sprinting through the jungle with Cobb's thugs close on their heels.

"Halt! Stop! Cease!" Kalani barked.

"Just stop running!" pleaded Makala, gasping for breath.

Reaching the main road, Billy yelled, "Come on, come on! To the bike!"

Allie had barely climbed on and shoved the helmet on her head when Billy threw the bike into gear and took off. The thugs ran toward them, and Makala dove for the bike as they pulled away. He missed, hitting the dirt with a thud. Billy quickly throttled the bike to the max.

Two more of Cobb's men jumped into a nearby black jeep as Kalani screamed, "Get them!"

Billy turned onto the main road and headed down the mountainside, pursued by the jeep, which was rapidly gaining ground.

Suddenly Billy cut right, jumping his bike off the road and onto a dirt path, leaving the jeep behind. The bike bounced along, forcing its riders to duck low-hanging vines and branches, leaves slapping at their faces and arms. But as they cleared the trees and came back out on the road, the Jeep caught up, roaring at them from the side.

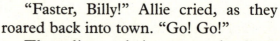

"Faster, Billy!" Allie cried, as they roared back into town. "Go! Go!"

Threading their way between buildings and down narrow alleys, they struggled to shake off the jeep.

"Look out!" Allie screamed as a motorcycle crossed the road in front of them. Billy swerved, narrowly avoiding it. The jeep also swerved, but then lost control. Spinning wildly, the jeep crashed into a roadside food stand, knocking over the grill and sending an explosion high into the sky. Billy skidded to a stop to watch as the two men inside the jeep bailed out, cursing their bad luck.

Grateful for their escape, Billy and Allie zoomed off.

At Billy's house, they jumped off the bike and hurried up to the door.

"I can't wait to see the look on your dad's face," Allie said, practically bouncing with anticipation. "He's gonna be so excited!"

"I know!" Billy said. "Oh, wait . . . wait." He dug the

medallion out of his pack and was about
to put it around his neck, when he heard
Allie gasp.

"Billy . . . what is that?" she asked,
pointing at his pocket, which had begun
to glow with an eerie blue light.

Billy looked down, puzzled. Seeing
the light, he reached into his pocket and pulled out the
stone his mother had given him. He'd completely forgotten about it. Holding the stone in his hand, he watched in
amazement as it soared into the air, the sooty black covering dissolving away to reveal a beautiful blue stone. The
stone glowed brighter, spun, and then glided into place,
sealing itself inside the medallion.

Allie gasped. "Oh . . . wow!"

"The stone!" Billy exclaimed. "It really is special, just
like my mom said! Allie, come on. We've got to show my
dad."

Allie grabbed Billy's arm as he started to run inside the
house. "Wait!" she said. "You should put it on! You should
surprise him."

"Yeah!" Billy placed the medallion around his neck,
tucked it inside his vest, and zipped it up.

Opening the front door, Billy stopped suddenly. A broken vase lay on the floor just inside the doorway. Peering
over Billy's shoulder, Allie spotted it too. Exchanging worried glances, the two friends started inside. On her way
in, Allie grabbed Faleaka's staff which had been leaning
against the wall.

*We just might need this,* she thought.

## Chapter 8

# The Wish

Billy and Allie stepped carefully over the broken vase, slipping quietly into the room. Suddenly Billy stopped, his breath caught in his chest.

*Dad!*

There before him, tied to a chair, was his father. Kalani stood next to him, smiling coldly, while Makala closed the door behind them, trapping them inside.

"'Tis good for a family to be together," Kalani said, fingering a huge knife.

Billy and Allie stood close together, saying nothing.

Makala laughed at them. "You gave us a good chase. Now, just gimme the medallion," he said moving toward them, his blood-red cobra tattoo standing out vividly on his arm.

Billy's dad shook his head in disbelief. "Are you guys nuts? He doesn't have the medallion," Dr. Stone said wearily.

"But, Dad . . ." Billy began.

"He's just a kid," Dr. Stone insisted. "I'm the archeologist here!"

Billy's eyes flashed with anger as the words sank in. Glaring at his father, he slowly pulled out the medallion.

Dr. Stone stared, open-mouthed, in surprise.

"He's more of an arco-lo-mol-ogist than you," Makala laughed, picking up a large machete. "Come on, kid, give it here!"

"No!" Billy shouted.

"You're going to wish you'd given it to us," Kalani said, moving toward Billy threateningly.

Allie placed a hand on Billy's shoulder. "Billy . . ."

Billy glared at them all. "You know what I wish?" he demanded, not noticing the blue light beginning to glow from the medallion. "I wish that this whole mess had never happened!"

With his last word, the stone seemed to explode with an unearthly blue light, followed by a massive peal of thunder, and then Billy and Allie vanished from sight.

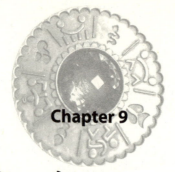

## Chapter 9

# Back in Time

*Aumakua Island, 1827, eight years after King Kieli's death...*

Billy and Allie stared, unbelieving, at the scene before them. They were no longer in Billy's living room. Instead, they were standing at the edge of a lush, tropical forest, looking out onto a beach filled with people.

"What just happened?" Allie asked, brushing the hair out of her face and clutching Faleaka's staff tightly.

Billy lifted the medallion and stared at it. "I can't believe it! It works!" he said, thunderstruck.

"Where *are* we?" Allie asked, looking around.

Billy let the medallion fall back to his chest and stared out at the people on the beach. Men were fishing with nets and spears—just like the one he'd found yesterday—while women carried baskets of fish and fruit, and children hunted for shells in the sand.

"Not *where*," Billy said, *"when."* Then, grinning, he added, "Allie, I think we're back in time."

"Billy, I know this may look good," Allie whispered anxiously, "but this is *really* not good."

"Relax!" Billy said.

"Wish us back right now," Allie pleaded. "I have a book I need to finish."

"You're kidding, right? We're actually witnessing history, which is *way* better than just reading about it. Besides, what could go wrong?"

Billy had barely gotten the words out of his mouth, when he felt a sharp jab in his back. Tucking the medallion back inside his vest, he turned around to see a chubby young warrior holding a fishing spear in one hand and a half-eaten mango in the other.

The young warrior glowered at them with as much fierceness as he could muster in a face that was more used to smiling than threatening.

"What could go wrong?" Allie asked, her voice shrill. "Oh, I don't know . . . what do you think?"

"Let's go," the young warrior mumbled, jabbing them with his spear and pointing toward a dirt trail. The prisoners walked quickly, wincing whenever he hurried them along with the point of his spear.

"We're friends . . . really!" Allie said. "What's your name?"

"I am Anui, warrior of King Huko," he replied self-importantly. "And you are my prisoners."

As the three entered the village, Billy and Allie were amazed by its simple beauty. Round huts made of bamboo and palm leaves encircled an open area. At the village's center stood a statue of a man. Billy recognized it as the one that now stood in the center of town. At the edge of the village, a series of small waterfalls cascaded down to a pool where children waded and women washed out clothing.

As Anui marched his prisoners into the village, people began to gather around, whispering and pointing curiously at the strangers.

"Allie! Allie, look!" Billy said, waving his hand out over the village. "We're seeing the actual village that my dad's been digging up all these years."

"I have a bad feeling about this, Billy," Allie said quietly.

"Come on, Allie. This is amazing!" Billy said.

"Are you kidding?" Allie said nervously, glancing around. "You know how it goes in the movies, right? Whenever people go back in time, things get messed up. Dinosaurs end up at the mall and stuff."

"We haven't gone *that* far back in time," Billy insisted.

Anui herded his prisoners to the village center, where they were quickly surrounded.

Allie looked at the villagers fearfully and turned to face Billy. "Wish us back! Wish us back right now!" she pleaded.

Just then, a voice called from behind the crowd. "Make way for the great Huko!"

Allie and Billy turned toward the voice just as a small boy stepped in front of them.

"Hey, there," Billy chuckled with relief, bending down to greet the boy.

"Oh! He's so cute!" Allie said, smiling for the first time.

Just then a tall, bronzed teen wearing a blue sash stepped up, pushing the small boy aside and giving Allie and Billy their first glimpse of King Huko.

Allie straightened up and nervously brushed the hair from her eyes. "Oh, he is *sooo* cute!" she giggled.

Billy shot her a look of disbelief mingled with disgust.

"Who are you?" Huko demanded as he eyed the prisoners suspiciously.

"I'm Billy, and this is Allie," he answered.

Allie waved a flirty "hi," and Billy rolled his eyes at her.

Their strange clothes fascinated Huko. He stepped forward and peered closely at the zipper on Billy's vest.

"Your robe has teeth," Huko proclaimed as he grabbed the zipper and tugged it down. Billy's vest fell open, revealing the medallion.

"The medallion . . . and the stone," Huko breathed in amazement, lifting it up off Billy's chest.

When the villagers saw the medallion, they began to cheer. Some even bowed to Billy and Allie!

Seeing his subjects' reactions made Huko jealous. There was no way he was going to bow to this imposter. Stepping closer, Huko was just about to snatch the medallion from around Billy's neck, when he realized that his anger might seem like weakness, so he decided to try a different approach.

"Well, you've found the medallion and brought it back to me," Huko said cunningly. "And look! He has also found the stone!"

Thrilled that the people's slavery to Cobra might actually end, one of village elders spoke up. "At last! We are saved! Our medallion has been returned by our new king!"

The crowd cheered, but Huko shook his head fiercely. "I am king," he said. Turning to face the villagers, he thumped his chest and shouted, "I am king!"

Ignoring him, the village elder bowed before Billy and said, "Please stay for dinner, our Most Honored Radiance."

"Me? An honored radiance?" Billy asked, starting to warm to this whole king idea.

The elder nodded, and Billy smiled.

"I'm sorry," Allie began, "but we really, *really* have to get back to . . ."

"We're staying! We're staying!" Billy interrupted, turning to the villagers and raising his staff high in the air for all to see.

The villagers broke into cheers again.

One look at Billy's face told Allie there would be no reasoning with him. "But only for dinner," she added.

The elder turned to the villagers and declared, "Tonight, we must celebrate! We shall have the visitors for dinner!"

Alarmed, Allie turned to Billy. "Does he mean they're gonna feed us . . . or eat us?" she asked.

# Chapter 10

# Betrayed!

Night fell on the village, erasing the glowing streaks of red, orange, and purple that had stretched across the sky. The usually somber village had been transformed into a place of celebration—their years of slavery to Cobra were about to end.

Torches blazed all around, throwing long shadows across the village and giving light to the men lunging and whirling through a ceremonial battle dance as drums beat out a steady, pounding rhythm. For the feast, women had prepared steaming hot loaves of bread, fresh fish, heaping platters of vegetables and fruits, and slabs of roasted meats. Hollowed out pineapples held the most delicious juice Billy and Allie had ever tasted. Flowers of every color had been strung into colorful leis for all to wear. Everyone ate and laughed and danced. The medallion had been returned—and soon, their years of slavery to Cobra would be no more!

Billy sat on Huko's throne, a blue sash of royalty now draped over his shoulders. Huko stood behind him, waiting for his chance to snatch the medallion.

As Billy watched the dancers, Huko leaned over his

shoulder and hissed, "I want my throne back—now!" He then straightened and smiled out at the villagers, pretending everything was fine.

"Lemme think about that," Billy said, rubbing his chin thoughtfully. "Hmm . . ."

At that moment, one of the village women stepped up to Billy, carrying a tray loaded with slices of fresh pineapples and mangos. Picking up a piece of fresh mango, she fed it to Billy.

As Billy chewed, he smiled back at Huko and shook his head saying, "I don't think so."

"You're no king," Huko growled.

Billy looked out over the celebrating villagers. "They think I am," he said smugly.

★ ★ ★

Meanwhile, Allie sat by herself near the waterfall, watching the celebration from a distance and wishing for home— even if home were only the orphanage. One of the islanders came and offered her a bamboo tray of food. Allie took the tray, thanking her. But when she looked down at it, her stomach lurched—it was filled with some sort of large, black, cooked beetles.

*Oh, gross!* she thought, trying not to gag.

At that moment, Anui came over and flopped down next to her. His cheerful smile was soon replaced by one of hungry interest as he pointed to the tray filled with beetles.

"Hey, you gonna eat those?" Anui asked hopefully.

"All yours," Allie said, shaking her head and handing him the tray. Then she watched in horror as he picked up a beetle and happily crunched off its head.

"Ugh!" she gasped and turned away, trying not to be sick.

Anui shrugged and kept eating. Though he took his service to King Huko seriously, his real interest was food—finding it, preparing it, and most especially, eating it. If the medallion had not been lost and his people enslaved, Anui would probably never have become a warrior. But life for everyone in the village had changed drastically after King Kieli's death. Much of the food they collected and prepared was taken back to Cobra Island—along with many of the villagers who were forced to work as Cobra's slaves. The people had not only lost their king and their freedom, they had also lost their hope. And Anui knew that—in spite of his arrogance—Huko still blamed himself for that terrible day.

*But things will be different now,* he thought, munching happily.

★ ★ ★

As Billy enjoyed the celebration, a beautiful young woman stepped up to him. Dressed in a simple wrap dress, she carried a bouquet of white flowers. Bowing slightly, she presented the flowers to Billy and said, "Thank you for returning the symbol of our worth. The music in our hearts plays once more."

Billy smiled. He was about to speak when Huko interrupted him.

"Mohea! You must not speak directly to our guests," he scolded.

"Some of us have never learned the true meaning of the royal medallion," she said, her dark eyes fixed on Huko.

Bowing again to Billy, Mohea started to turn away.

"Uh . . . wait! You're Mohea?" Billy asked.

The young woman nodded.

"I *love* your writings," Billy said.

"But . . . I don't write," she said, smiling and shaking her head in confusion.

"Trust me. You will," Billy said.

Mohea nodded, puzzled, and backed away slowly, returning to the celebration.

Billy sat back in his throne and looked out over the village—his village.

*I like being king,* he thought to himself.

★ ★ ★

Just as he had done all those years ago, when he had betrayed King Kieli, Cobra's spy slipped away from the festivities and darted through the jungle. Running down the overgrown path to the cliff, he pulled the drum out of its hiding place. Then he beat out the message, announcing the medallion's return.

Back in the village, no one heard the spy's message over the beating drums of their own celebration.

★ ★ ★

## On Cobra Island . . .

Across the ocean waters, but still within sight of Aumakua Island, Cobra Island loomed menacingly on the dark horizon. Its sharp, jagged cliffs of red, brown, and black were as harsh as its ruler. Cobra's fortress took up almost half the island, with part of it jutting out over the waters like the head of a snake ready to strike.

Inside the fortress, Cobra sat on his throne, deep in thought. Absentmindedly, he dipped the fang-like nails of his forefinger and thumb into the small bowl of poison that sat next to his throne. The poison hissed and sizzled. The guards standing next to his throne watched and swallowed nervously.

Suddenly, two warriors burst into the throne room and crossed the polished stone floor. They dropped to their knees, eyes lowered.

"The medallion, my lord, it has been found. And the stone too," the first warrior said. "The medallion is whole once more."

"How is this possible?" Cobra demanded, sitting upright. "We have dug a thousand holes without finding it. Where was it found?"

"A stranger brought it to them. They have made him their new king," the warrior answered nervously.

"*I* am their king!" Cobra shouted angrily, rising to his feet.

"They do not seem to remember that," the second warrior replied without thinking.

Cobra's eyes narrowed to snake-like slits, and he slowly descended the steps from the throne to face the man.

Realizing his mistake, the warrior bowed his head in fear, as sweat trickled down his face. "I . . . I meant no disrespect, my lord," he stammered.

Cobra nodded to the guard standing against the wall, near a lever. At Cobra's signal, he pulled the level, opening up the fiery Pit of Death.

The warrior who had so foolishly spoken stared at Cobra in horror and began to back away. But there was no escape. Smiling coldly, Cobra raised his hand and struck, the poisoned fangs of his fingernails digging into the man's neck. A wisp of smoke hissed up from the wound. Death was almost instantaneous, but not before the man felt Cobra push him over the edge and into the flames of the pit.

Turning back to the first warrior, Cobra ordered, "Prepare the boats. We invade."

"Yes, my lord," the warrior answered and hurried out of the room, relieved to be away from his master.

# Chapter 11

# The Invasion

*On Aumakua Island . . .*

Not long after sunrise the next morning, Huko led Billy, Allie, and Anui on a walk around the island. Billy was amazed at how different everything looked. It was incredible to see all the places that he and his dad had explored over the years as they had originally been.

The four of them crossed over the shallow waters at the top of a gentle waterfall. The rocks were slippery and Anui—never the best at balance—stumbled repeatedly, while Billy steadied himself with Faleaka's staff.

As Allie reached the other side and struggled to step up onto the bank, Huko turned and offered her his hand, helping her up.

"You're very kind," she said, smiling shyly.

"And you are very beautiful," Huko replied. Bending down, he plucked a nearby flower and slipped it behind Allie's ear, causing Allie to blush.

Billy watched them, his chest feeling oddly tight.

★ ★ ★

While the kids explored, Cobra's fleet of sleek canoes slipped onto the shore of Aumakua Island. As soon as his men were gathered around him, Cobra nodded to one of his generals. The general waved his arm high in the air, signaling his men to attack. Fanning out, Cobra's warriors slipped silently through the trees and toward the village.

Knowing that the medallion had been found in one piece, Cobra planned to catch the villagers by surprise, before they could use the medallion against him. Crawling across open areas and darting from tree to tree, his warriors hid whenever they spotted an unsuspecting villager.

Reaching the village, they quickly surrounded it. At Cobra's signal, they attacked without warning. Women and children ran screaming toward the jungle as the men grabbed up anything they could use for a weapon. One man pulled a log from the fire, raising its flaming end high above his head to strike. But he quickly dropped it as he felt the cold point of a spear pressed against his back. Cobra had given strict orders not to kill the villagers unnecessarily. He had other plans for his slaves.

★ ★ ★

Crossing over the top of another waterfall, this one much higher, Huko and the others were completely unaware of what was happening back in the village.

Suddenly, Huko turned on Billy and pointed at his chest. "I know the medallion brought you here. Give it to me!" he demanded.

Billy just shook his head. "No."

"I am Huko!" he shouted. "I am the son of King Kieli. The medallion should only be worn by the island's rightful king."

"No," Billy said again, stepping back a couple of paces. "You know, I'm beginning to think the medallion wants *me* to be king. Maybe because *I* won't lose it!"

"We don't talk about that," Anui said nervously.

"In my great mercy, I will forgive you," Huko warned.

Billy smirked at him. "You'll forgive me? Come on, Allie," he said, turning away from Huko, "let's go back to *my* village."

Billy and Allie started back across the falls and toward the village, but Huko stormed after them, stopping them halfway across.

"Give me the medallion!" he demanded, grabbing Billy's shoulder and spinning him around to face him.

"No!" Billy shouted, throwing Huko's hand off him.

"It's mine!" Huko shouted.

"I don't think so!" Billy spat back, taking the medallion from around his neck and holding it tightly in his hand.

"I lost my father over that medallion," Huko shot back.

"So did I!" Billy shouted angrily.

Allie took a couple of steps back, looking desperately from one boy to the other. "You know what? Just stop it! Okay?" Allie pleaded. "Just stop fight . . ."

Suddenly, an icy hand gripped the back of her neck. Allie froze.

"*This* is a king?" Cobra sneered, looking Billy up and down.

Billy turned, horrified to see the man holding his best friend. Even though he'd seen drawings of Cobra, he was far more terrifying in person than in any picture, and the guards with him were almost as frightening.

"I believe you have something *I* want," Cobra demanded, holding out his hand and ignoring Huko.

Billy held the medallion behind his back as he stared with sick fascination at the two sharpened fangs on the ends of Cobra's fingers. He remembered with a shiver the legend of their poison and wondered if Allie were about to become their next victim.

As Billy tried to figure out what to do, Huko slipped up behind him, snatched the medallion from his hand, and raised it high in the air, shouting at Cobra, "I banish you!"

Huko's words brought a startled look from everyone and a twinge of fear to the eyes of Cobra's warriors, but nothing happened. The stone did not glow. There was no flash, no noise. The stone remained cold and quiet in its setting.

Fear and disbelief flashed across the young king's face. Why hadn't the medallion worked? Glancing at it quickly for fear that the stone was once again lost, Huko noted with relief that it was still there.

Cobra slowly smiled, realizing that Huko was unable to make the medallion work. "The medallion!" he demanded. "Give it to me!"

Recovering from his shock, Billy sprang into action. He

snatched the medallion back from Huko. With more brav-
ery and determination than he had ever felt, he lifted the
medallion over his head and started to put it on.

"Stop . . . or she dies!" Cobra shouted.

"I told you just to wish us back!" Allie cried.

Billy hesitated. He didn't know why the medallion
hadn't worked for Huko. All he knew for sure was that
Cobra had Allie—and that meant Cobra was in control.

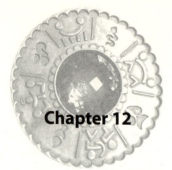

## Chapter 12

# Cobra Takes Control

"Let her go, and I'll give it to you," Billy said.

Cobra had never seen Billy before, and from the way he was dressed beneath the royal sash, the boy did not appear to be from any of the nearby islands, which made him wonder why these outsiders would interfere in his affairs. Instead of freeing Allie, he tightened his grip on her throat, the poisoned fang of his finger ready to strike.

Allie trembled. Having spent her life buried in books, she knew the danger of Cobra's poison.

"First, the medallion," Cobra insisted, giving Billy a warning look.

Allie's eyes pleaded silently with Billy.

Believing that Cobra would not allow one of his warriors

to catch the medallion, Billy threw it high into the air. Cobra let go of Allie to grab for it, and she ran over to join Billy, Huko, and Anui at the top of the waterfall.

As Cobra caught the medallion, a look of triumph filled his face. Billy leaned slightly over the edge of the waterfall, peering down at the crashing, foaming waters plunging over a hundred feet into the deep pool. It was their only chance at escape.

"Jump!" he cried.

Together, the four kids leapt over the side, disappearing into the waters below.

"I wish you dead!" Cobra screamed after them, holding the medallion high in the air. Looking down, he saw no sign of his enemies. He knew that if the fall hadn't killed them, his wish had.

Satisfied, Cobra returned to the village in triumph. His trophy, now firmly in place around his neck, told the people all they needed to know: he was their king and he held all the power. Just when they thought they would finally be free again, they lost not only the medallion, but also their new king.

As Cobra passed by Mohea, she glared up at him defiantly, but he just laughed at her. He had nothing to fear from such as these.

"If you thought it was difficult being my slaves before, you were mistaken," Cobra threatened. "I have been too easy on you. Now you will know what it truly means to be my slaves."

Grabbing one of his warriors, Cobra ordered, "Take more slaves back to Cobra Island. They will replace the ones who have died."

"Yes, my lord," the warrior answered, bowing deeply.

"And where are my trackers?"

"Trackers!" the warrior called.

Two men appeared from the far edges of the village. Had Billy and Allie seen these two, they would have recognized them instantly. The two men could have been the twins of Cobb's thugs, Kalani and Makala—they were, in fact, their ancestors. Even their names were similar—Kalanu, and Makawa. Dressed in the sealskin vest and scarlet pants that marked them as one of Cobra's warriors, each of them carried a deadly sharp machete.

"Bring me the dead bodies of the four who defied me," Cobra ordered. "I wish to display them as a warning to all who would disobey me."

"With hearty dispatch, my lord," said the thin tracker named Kalanu.

"You got it, Cobe," answered Makawa, earning him a glare of disapproval from Cobra.

★ ★ ★

Sometime later, Allie began to stir, her muscles aching all over. Opening her eyes, she found herself lying at the water's edge. Sitting up, she discovered Huko and Billy sprawled out next to her.

Grateful to still be breathing, she got to her feet and began shaking Billy and Huko. They awoke coughing and sputtering.

"We did it! You guys, we did it!" she said. "We're alive! We're alive!"

Stretching, Billy staggered to his feet and looked around. "Hey, where's Anui?"

They searched the area, calling Anui's name in low voices and growing fearful.

"He's gotta be here somewhere," Billy insisted. "Search the other bank."

They checked every inch of ground, but Anui was nowhere to be found.

"He was a loyal subject," Huko said aloud, sounding dazed, as the full impact of the loss hit him.

"How did Cobra know we had the medallion?" Allie asked.

"Obviously, a traitor is still within our midst," Huko replied.

"You mean you never found out who betrayed your father the first time?" Allie asked, remembering the legend.

"I would have thought he'd returned to Cobra Island long ago to live the good life," Billy added.

"The only one living the 'good life' is Cobra. He takes our food and enslaves my people. They spend most of their lives deep in his dungeons. Their families do not see them until they either grow too old or too sick to work. Then they are sent back to the village to die."

"That's horrible!" Allie cried.

"Even worse than in our time," Billy agreed.

"What is 'your time' you speak of? Where do you come from?" Huko demanded.

"We are your . . . future," Allie said, struggling to think of a way to explain. "Actually, Billy is your great, great, great, great . . . grandson. Not sure if that's enough greats."

"How is this possible?" Huko asked.

"The medallion sent us back in time," Billy explained.

"Then the medallion worked for you?"

"Nobody was more surprised than I was. Look, I don't know why it didn't obey you," Billy said, "but it does work . . . or at least it did."

Huko shook his head. "It must be me. It does not accept me as the rightful king."

"It doesn't matter anymore anyway," Billy said. "Anui is dead, and Cobra has the medallion."

The thought of Anui dead brought fresh tears to Allie's eyes. She glared at Billy.

"I told you to wish us back right away."

At that moment, Anui strolled up behind them, munching a papaya. He had no idea why Allie was so upset, but her sadness worried him. "Why are you crying?" he asked.

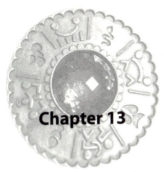

## Chapter 13

# A Spoiled Brat

"Anui!" Allie cried, throwing her arms around him and hugging him. "We thought you were dead!"

"Um, I was just getting a snack. After pulling you guys out of the river, I was kinda hungry," he said shyly.

"*You* pulled us out of the river?" Huko asked, surprised.

"How else did you think you got out?" Anui asked. Then, holding out a piece of fruit, he offered, "Want some?" When no one took any, he shrugged and asked, "Now what do we do?"

Getting back to business, Billy turned to Huko and said, "We *have* to go after the medallion."

"Yes!" Huko said fiercely. "We'll attack Cobra Island and take back the medallion."

"Wait a minute!" Billy said. "How exactly do we do that? There's one, two, three, four of us," he said, pointing

Faleaka's staff at each of them in turn, "and like, an entire army of them. We can't just attack—that's a stupid idea!"

Infuriated, Huko demanded, "Who do you think you're talking to?"

"A spoiled brat," Billy said icily.

"He's right," Anui agreed.

"What?" Huko said, turning on Anui.

"Not that you are a spoiled brat," Anui explained quickly, "but that we can't do this alone,"

"The only chance we have is with Faleaka," Billy said.

Huko and Anui looked at Billy with pity.

"No one has seen Faleaka since my father's death," Huko said, shaking his head. "He's dead."

"I'm telling you, he's alive. He just went off to live by himself," Billy declared.

"He is dead!" Huko insisted.

"Well, my father and I have been to his hidden hut many times. Look, it's marked right here on my map." Billy dropped to the ground and spread out his map. "See for yourself."

"If he *is* alive, then he's a coward," Huko said fiercely.

Billy's expression turned stubborn. "He was your father's most trusted advisor. We're going to find Faleaka and see what he thinks we should do."

"We *go* to Cobra's island," Huko insisted.

"No! We go to find Faleaka!" and with that Billy wheeled around and began walking off in the direction of Faleaka's hut. Not knowing what else to do, Allie followed.

Huko glared after them. He truly believed that Faleaka was dead, but he knew he couldn't face Cobra with just

Map of Aumakua Island

Billy Stone

Billy's best friend, Allie

Billy's father, archaeologist
Dr. Michael Stone

Billy and Allie, figuring it out

Faleaka, the legend begins

Shut down by Cobb

Mr. Cobb, descendant of the evil
King Cobra

Finding the medallion

The medallion

Mohea

A new king?

Cobra searches for the medallion

Cobra attacks Aumakua Island

Billy and Huko confront Cobra

Billy and Cobra fight for the medallion

The caves of Cobra Island

Trackers search for Billy

Slaves from Aumakua Island

King Cobra

Faleaka, the wise man

Trackers!

Watching and waiting

Trapped!

Trapped in the cell

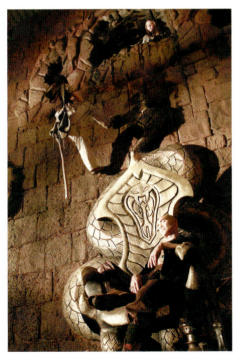

A brave attempt to take back the medallion

"Tonight . . . we destroy our enemies!"

King Cobra watches
the celebration

Allie is taken prisoner!

Stuck in the past?

himself and Anui, so—reluctantly—he stomped off after Billy.

Happy that they were all at least going in the same direction, Anui followed.

★ ★ ★

Loaded with captives, Cobra's canoes sped swiftly over the waves. Mohea sat in one of the boats, her wrists bound tightly. Silent tears ran down her cheeks, as she watched her beloved Aumakua Island disappear into the distance. She knew her life would now be filled with backbreaking labor and constant hunger, but she was determined to survive and to somehow find a way home.

*Until then,* she thought, *perhaps I can find a way to help my people.*

★ ★ ★

Seated in the lead boat, Cobra stared down at the medallion, tracing its carvings with a finger. He had searched for the medallion for so long and now it was finally his.

*Nothing can stop me now,* he thought. *Nothing!*

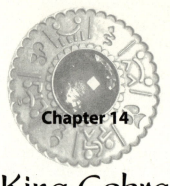

## Chapter 14

# King Cobra

**_Back on Cobra Island . . ._**

The doors to Cobra's throne room swung open, revealing rows of powerful warriors standing in tight formation. As Cobra stepped into the room, two warriors began beating out a steady rhythm on two large drums, while the rest chanted loudly: "King Cobra! King Cobra! King Cobra!"

Dressed in his best silken robes of deep, blood red, Cobra strode proudly through the midst of his warriors and up to his throne. The medallion gleamed on his chest for all to see.

As Cobra seated himself on his throne, one of his top generals dropped to one knee before him and said, "Now you are truly invincible, my lord."

Cobra offered the general his hand to be kissed.

Swallowing his revulsion, the general pressed his lips to Cobra's cold, dry hand with its poisoned fingertips. It was like kissing the head of a snake.

★ ★ ★

*On Aumakua Island, at the bottom of the falls . . .*

Kalanu bent down and studied the riverbank, noting the multiple footprints in the mud.

"They yet live!" he exclaimed.

"How do you know?" Makawa asked.

"The true question is not, *How do I know?* Rather, the question is—as always—*How do you not know?*" snipped Kalanu. Then he began pointing out the signs. "Broken branches, forty-four footfalls on the muddied bank, a tree bruised by someone's passing, and a partially eaten fruit harvested this day."

Makawa picked up the half-eaten mango and took a bite. "If you say so."

"You are pathetic!" Kalanu screeched, throwing up his hands in frustration. "This way!" he said, stomping off in the direction of the kids' tracks.

# Chapter 15

# The Search for Faleaka

Billy and the others walked along the edge of a narrow river, following an overgrown path that wound through patches of dense jungle trees and foliage. Billy searched the terrain for the landmarks on his map—but much had changed over the centuries.

Rounding a bend, the four found themselves suddenly staring up at the side of steep cliff.

"It's a dead end," Allie said, disappointed.

"You've led us the wrong way," Huko accused.

"I am *not* wrong," Billy said calmly. "I know this cliff. It's right here on my map, and Faleaka lives up there," he said, pointing to the top of the cliff.

Huko looked at Billy doubtfully, then said, "First one to the top is king," and sprinted to the cliff, climbing upward as fast as he could.

"What?" Billy exclaimed, not believing what Huko had said. "Wait! You didn't even say go!"

Turning to Allie, he complained, "He didn't even say go!" Then throwing down the staff, Billy sped off after Huko.

Allie picked up the staff and looked around for a safer way to the top: she did not want to make the dangerous climb. Spotting an easier route, she called out, "Hey, Anui! There's a path over there." Then calling up to Huko and Billy, she said, "Hey, you guys! You guys! There's a path over here."

But Billy and Huko were too busy climbing to hear her.

Allie shook her head in disgust. "Come on, Anui," she said, and they started up the path.

As the two boys jostled their way up the cliff, Billy suddenly slipped, scraping his arm as he grappled for a ledge. A jolt of fear rippled through him.

Huko looked back down at Billy as he struggled to regain his footing, but he refused to go back and help.

A short time later, Huko's own foot became wedged in a tight crevice. As he twisted and turned, trying to free himself, Billy passed him by. Huko freed himself and bolted after Billy. In their race to the top, the boys became reckless, climbing faster and faster.

With his longer arms and legs, Huko soon took the lead again, but Billy stayed close. When Huko accidentally dislodged a boulder, it bounced down the side of the cliff, narrowly missing Billy's head. Billy slipped and slid several feet down the rock face until his hand caught hold of a thick root.

Panting, Billy rested a moment while he caught his breath and brought his fear under control. Looking up he spotted Huko far above. Anger replaced fear as he once more began climbing as fast as he could, throwing caution to the wind.

Huko was now only a few feet from the top. But as he brought his right leg up to the next foothold, the rock he stood on crumbled and Huko fell.

## Chapter 16

# Faleaka?

As Huko slid past him, Billy reached out and grabbed his arm. Huko's weight jerked Billy hard, nearly pulling him down, as well. As he struggled to keep his grip, Huko kicked at the rock face until he found a foothold. White-faced with fear, neither moved for several seconds, then Huko grinned and continued his climb.

With a burst of speed, Billy went after him. Somehow pulling ahead by inches, Billy slapped his hand down on the top of the cliff first. A split second later, Huko catapulted past him, planting his foot next to Billy's hand. Billy finished pulling himself up and the two stood panting and glaring at each other.

"Ha!" Billy crowed, gasping for air. "I am king because my hand touched down first!"

"No!" Huko shouted. "Your hand does not count. It has to be a foot. I am king!" he said, thumping his chest.

Turning away from the cliff, the two arguing boys almost ran into Allie and Anui, who had been waiting for them at the top.

"How'd you get up here so fast?" Billy asked, as Allie returned Faleaka's staff to him.

"Allie found a nice path. Much easier," Anui grinned.

Huko looked around the small clearing surrounded by thick bushes, trees, and shrubs. "Look," he said, "there's nothing here. Faleaka doesn't live here! He's dead . . . and I am king."

While the boys continued to argue, Allie explored the clearing. Suddenly she called out, "Look, you guys!"

The boys joined her, looking around and trying to see what it was that she found so interesting.

"Look," she said, pointing to bushes loaded with berries, "these wouldn't be growing here naturally like this—especially not in such neat rows. Someone has planted them here."

"She reads a lot," Billy explained to the others, who were looking at her curiously.

Allie continued searching the area. Pushing through a narrow opening in some bushes, she disappeared from sight. Billy and the others followed. On the other side, they found Allie smiling and pointing at a small, patched and weathered hut, nestled in a cluster of palm trees. Colorful wild flowers were planted around its edges, and to one side, a small garden grew vegetables and herbs. Wooden wind chimes tinkled softly in the breeze. A pot hung over a fire pit, with something delicious smelling bubbling inside it.

"You found it!" Billy grinned. "Come on," he said, leading the others forward.

"Mmm, something smells good," Anui added.

Billy went straight to the door of the small hut and knocked. No one answered. Pushing the door open slowly, he stepped into the empty hut, but a voice stopped him.

"Shouldn't you be invited first?" asked a voice from behind them.

Startled, the four turned to see an old man with stringy, dark hair and weathered, brown skin.

"We're looking for Faleaka," Billy told him.

The man narrowed his eyes at his visitors. His clothes were shabby and worn, but neat. Grunting, he hobbled past them, slamming the door in Billy's face. They could hear him mumbling inside the hut.

Billy yelled through the door, "Do you know where he is?"

His question was answered with more mumbling.

"Crazy old man," Huko muttered.

"Guess we'll have to keep looking," Allie concluded.

"Let's go," Billy agreed. "Faleaka has to be around here somewhere."

"I'm telling you, he is dead," Huko said firmly.

As the kids turned to leave, the door of the hut suddenly flew open.

"What are you waiting for? A written invitation? Come on in!" the old man said.

Billy, Allie, Huko, and Anui exchanged wary glances before stepping inside. The interior of the hut was sparsely furnished—a bed, some shelves, and a large table with some rough-hewn benches.

"Sit," the hut's owner said, pointing toward the table. He sat, as well, hunching over and beginning to work on the intricate carvings of a large staff.

Billy took a seat near the old man, watching him closely. Huko, Anui, and Allie also sat down.

Finally, the old man asked, "Why do you seek Faleaka?"

"We need his help," Billy said.

The old man hummed and whistled until finally, Huko could stand it no longer. He jumped up. "We're wasting time," he said impatiently, ready to storm out of the hut.

The man moved his walking stick, catching Billy's attention so that he noticed the carvings. A hawk! Looking at the staff that he carried, Billy recognized the same hawk—it was the same staff!

"Of course!" Billy said. "You're Faleaka!"

But the old man did not look up from his carving.

"Look at him! He is old and weak. He can't help us," Huko said.

Ignoring him, Billy continued, "Faleaka, we need your help to . . ."

". . . to regain the medallion," Faleaka finished, still not looking up from his carving.

Suddenly, Faleaka's face hardened. "Leave!" he said, pointing at the door. "Go back to the village. I will not help you."

"But we need your help," Billy begged.

"I will not help someone to their death," Faleaka said, looking Billy in the eye before turning back to his carving.

Billy's heart sank.

"I told you he can't help us," Huko hissed.

Bewildered, Billy tried once more. "My dad would have wanted me to come to you for your wisdom."

Faleaka looked at Billy briefly, sadly, before turning away yet again. "Go back now," Faleaka said.

"We can't go back," Billy shouted, frustrated. "There's nowhere to go to. The village is under Cobra's control. "And you wanna know what history says about you? You die alone, cowering up here while your village suffered in slavery."

"History cannot be changed," Faleaka answered in a voice filled with sadness.

"But it *can* be changed if you'll just help us," Billy pleaded.

"I will not help you die," Faleaka repeated stubbornly.

Growing angry, Billy said, "We're going after the medallion . . . with or without your help. So if we die, it will be because you didn't help us."

Faleaka's shoulders drooped. But then he started to laugh! Quiet at first, his laughter grew louder and louder.

"Well," he said, shaking his head, "perhaps it is time for all our stories to change. I guess it is better to fight like a tiger than to live like a kitty cat. I like you," he chuckled, pointing at Billy. "And I used to be like you . . . once upon a time. All right, I'll help you."

Billy's hopes soared, but Huko was furious. He stormed outside and the others followed him into the clearing.

"Bah! I tell you, he's a useless old man," Huko shouted. "And I'll prove it."

Huko was determined to defeat the man he felt had deserted him and his father. Grabbing up a thick branch from the ground, he turned and faced Faleaka.

"If you're such a great warrior," Huko challenged, "then fight me and prove it."

"No! Huko, you can't," Allie shouted. "Can't you see he's an old man?"

But when Allie tried to step between Faleaka and Huko, the old man gently moved her away. Holding his own staff with both hands, Faleaka prepared to fight.

Huko struck first, lunging forward, but his blow was instantly blocked by Faleaka's staff. He tried again, from the side, but was blocked again. Huko swung, jabbed, and kicked, but each time Faleaka blocked his blows. Then, without warning, Faleaka charged, striking Huko on the back of his legs and dropping him to his knees. Another quick blow to his back left Huko sprawled face first in the dirt. Faleaka planted his staff on the young kid's back.

"Yield," Faleaka demanded. He had no intention of really harming the boy; he only wanted to teach him a little lesson in humility.

Huko suddenly remembered watching his own father, King Kieli, sparring with Faleaka. He could still hear his father's laughter as he said, "I yield, Faleaka! I yield."

Brushing aside an unwanted tear, Huko whispered, "I yield."

Faleaka offered his hand to Huko, pulling the boy to his feet—just as he had done for King Kieli so many years before.

Standing before Faleaka, Huko looked him in the eye and asked, "So what do we do now?"

## Chapter 17

# The Slave Camp

*On Cobra Island . . .*

Inside his fortress, Cobra paced back and forth across his bed chamber. It was a lavish room, though cold and forbidding. In one corner stood a small fountain, its waters tumbling into a jet black basin. Across from it, Cobra's bed loomed—a massive wooden thing, wildly carved with coiling and striking snakes. A huge mirror filled much of one wall. Cobra stopped before it and stared at his reflection, admiring the medallion.

In the fireplace, a copper pot dangled over the flames, melted wax bubbling inside it. Cobra motioned to a nearby warrior who removed the pot and poured its wax into a shallow metal tray. Cobra took the medallion and pressed it into the hardening wax. Once the wax was set, he pulled the medallion out, leaving its imprint behind.

"The medallion must never be lost again, so I will seal it against my heart," Cobra told the warrior. "Have a breastplate made for the medallion."

Taking the wax imprint, the warrior bowed deeply, and left.

Cobra turned to a corner of the room where a large, partially completed painting of the medallion hung in a wooden frame. Picking up a brush, Cobra began to work, skillfully recreating the image of the medallion. But his cold smile did little to hide his terrible thoughts as he imagined the way to use the medallion and to make the people of Aumakua Island suffer.

★ ★ ★

Far beneath Cobra's feet, the slaves from Aumakua Island toiled in the maze of caves beneath his fortress. Forced to make weapons for Cobra's army, many labored over hot furnaces, melting the metal. The air was hot and heavy, making it difficult to breath. The caves rang with the hammer of metal on metal as slaves shaped the knives and swords. The only light came from the flames of the torches and furnaces.

Here and there, in corners of the caves, hammocks were strung between rocks. The slaves took turns resting so that the work of making weapons never stopped, day or night. Cobra, it seemed, had big plans for his army. His warriors constantly patrolled the caves—though the villagers didn't dare try to escape, knowing the caves were filled with deadly traps.

Exhausted, Mohea knelt before one of the furnaces, softening a piece of metal in its flames, before shaping it with her hammer. Looking up, she saw one of Cobra's men standing over her. Handing her the wax impression, he ordered, "Cobra wants a breastplate made to hold the medallion."

"Let him make it himself," Mohea snapped defiantly, tossing the wax impression aside.

The warrior's reaction was swift. Grabbing her by the arm, he placed the tip of his sword under her chin.

Mohea glared up at him bravely, "I am not afraid of you."

"Perhaps not . . ."

Mohea watched as the man's eyes shifted away from her, searching. Then he spotted an elderly woman, struggling with a load of wood.

"But perhaps *she* will be afraid of me," he threatened, pointing his sword at the old woman. "Your defiance will cause her death."

Terrified, the old woman stumbled, her load of wood falling to the floor. Jerking her arm free, Mohea ran to her, putting herself between the woman and the warrior.

"If you hurt any of my people," Mohea said coolly, "I will never make the breastplate for the medallion."

Mohea's threat was real—she knew she was the only slave capable of making such a breastplate. She had learned the skill from her mother, who—years before—had helped King Kieli first form the medallion.

Mohea watched the man waver. He knew he needed Mohea. If she refused to make the breastplate, it would not only mean her death, but most likely his, as well.

Knowing he was beaten, the warrior snarled, "You haven't heard the last of this." Then he turned and left the caves.

Mohea helped the older woman over to a rock where she could sit down, smiling at her small triumph.

# Chapter 18

# The Pineapple Strategy

**On Aumakua Island . . .**

Faleaka led the kids back toward his hut. Clearing his throat, he said, "Answer this: *'Atop his head, he wears a crown, above the village looking down. Beneath the soil his soul is born. An island king, when so adorned. Hard, yet soft; short, yet tall; through wisdom's patience, loved by all.'* What is it?"

Billy and the others looked at each other, completely baffled.

"Crazy old man," Huko said, his newfound respect quickly disappearing.

"A king?" Allie guessed.

Faleaka shook his head.

"A bird—with big feathers on its head?" Billy offered.

"Definitely . . . not." Turning to Anui, he said, "It is now left to you, young one."

"Is it . . . is it a-a . . . pineapple?" Anui guessed.

A huge smile spread across Faleaka's face. "Well done, my friend," he said. "Now we eat."

Faleaka pointed the four of them toward the pot still simmering over the fire. After dishing out a heaping bowl to each of them, Faleaka and his guests sat beneath the trees with their food. Everyone ate hungrily, except Huko who had much to think about and whose pride was still stinging.

As they finished their meal, Faleaka reached over and picked up three pineapples. He held one of them high in the air. "Behold . . . the way you will defeat Cobra," he announced.

"I told you he's crazy," Huko muttered, shaking his head.

Billy rolled his eyes at Huko, but privately wondered if he might be right.

Faleaka pretended not to notice. "Allie, I want you to make your pineapple explode," he said, handing her one of the pineapples, along with some empty drawstring pouches.

"Explode?" Allie asked incredulously. "How do I do that?"

"That is for you to decide," he said, tapping his forehead. "Think carefully."

"Anui," he said, holding up the second pineapple, "I want you to split your pineapple into two parts. Make one half taste as good as you can, and make the other half taste as bad as you can."

He rolled the pineapple to the boy and gave him two pouches before tossing the last pineapple to Huko.

"Huko, I want you to cut this pineapple into one hundred pieces. Each piece must be exactly the same size."

"We don't have time for games. We have a war to fight," Huko snarled.

"And a pineapple will lead you to victory," Faleaka assured him.

"What about Billy?" Allie asked, noticing that there was no pineapple left for him.

"It's okay," Billy assured her. Like Huko, he couldn't see how a pineapple was going to help them defeat Cobra's army.

"It's up in that tree," Faleaka told him, pointing to the top of a nearby coconut palm tree. "Billy, get me that pineapple."

Billy looked up and spotted a lone pineapple nestled among the coconuts. He wondered how on earth it had gotten up there . . . and how on earth he would get it down.

"Come back to me when you are ready," Faleaka finished. Then he went back to his hut and to his carving.

★ ★ ★

Allie stared at her pineapple, searching her memory for anything she'd ever read about making things explode. Then, she smiled. *It just might work,* she thought, jumping up.

Allie hurried over to the rocks scattered around the cliff, searching for a sharp stone to use as a tool. Finding what she wanted, she then made her way to a hot stream not far from the hut. She had spotted it earlier in their search for Faleaka. Allie knew from her chemistry books that this would be to find sulfur.

When she reached the steamy water, her nose wrinkled at the rotten egg smell. Spotting some yellow, blocky crystals, she scooped up a few and placed them in one of the pouches Faleaka had given her. Next, she needed potassium nitrate. Remembering a small cave along the path that she and Anui had taken to the top of the cliff, she headed there. Entering the cave, she saw several sparkling encrustations of niter—the mineral form of potassium nitrate—on the walls and ceilings of the cavern.

Using the sharp stone, she chipped off a few pieces and placed them in a second bag. Now all she needed was some charcoal, and she knew exactly where to find that— the coals of Faleaka's fire. Using the rock, she carefully scraped some out to cool, and then placed them in a third bag.

Allie then took the pouches over to a large, flat rock and spread out the ingredients. Trading her sharp stone for a rounder, flatter one, she carefully ground each one into a fine powder, keeping them separated, and returning the finished products to their original bags. Allie then borrowed Billy's knife to cut a hole in the top of her pineapple and hollow it out. She carefully poured a small amount of each powder inside and replaced the top, adding a small fuse made of vine.

Meanwhile, Anui searched the jungle for the ingredients he would need. Spotting a bush bursting with small, ripe, purple berries, he began to fill his pouch with the berries. He knew the village women often used the berries to make a rich, purple dye, but he also knew they were so bitter that no one ever ate them.

Next, Anui looked for sugarcane. As he searched, he spotted another berry, large and yellowish. This berry, he knew, could be used to make a powerful sleeping potion. But since Anui guessed that Faleaka did not wish to take a nap just now, he left those where they were. Finding the sugarcane, he cut some with his knife and stuffed it into the other pouch, then headed back to the clearing. Finding a comfortable place to work, Anui began mashing the sugarcane, squeezing its sweet juice on one half of his pineapple. After crushing the berries, he smeared them on the other half.

Huko sat nearby, cutting his pineapple into small, precise pieces. Angry and bored, he measured each piece against the next. His only amusement was watching Billy's failed attempts to climb the coconut palm, each attempt ending with him sliding back down the trunk.

With their tasks completed, the kids gathered around Faleaka—all except Billy who had given up trying to climb the tree and was now sitting next to it, his head hanging down in defeat.

Faleaka walked over to him and whispered quietly, "The answer is with you."

"I'm the problem, Faleaka, not the answer," Billy said, without looking up.

"The answer is with you," Faleaka repeated before returning to sit by the fire.

Billy sighed, stood up, and tried again. This time, he managed to make it about ten feet up the tree . . . before sliding back down and landing with a thud yet again.

Huko's laughter rang out across the clearing. Frustrated, Billy smacked his hand on the ground, hitting his pack.

*His pack!* Billy had an idea. Digging into his pack, he pulled out his slingshot. Smiling broadly, he picked up a small rock and fitted it into the sling. Taking aim, he fired at the pineapple, knocking it out of the tree and into his waiting hands. He walked over to where Faleaka waited with the others by the fire and handed him the pineapple.

Faleaka smiled, then said to Allie. "Show us your pineapple," he said.

Allie carried her pineapple a few feet away. Lighting one of the matches that Billy always kept in his pack for emergencies, she lit the fuse and quickly sprinted away.

*KA-BOOM!*

Pineapple chunks flew everywhere.

"It worked!" Allie shouted with delight. "It really worked!"

Next, Faleaka picked up the sweetened half of Anui's pineapple and tasted it.

"Mmm . . . very nice," he said, smacking his lips in pleasure as Anui watched, beaming.

"Now it's time for the other half." Faleaka picked it up and bit off a small piece. His face twisted into a grimace and his stomach heaved as he quickly spat it out again.

"That is truly terrible," Faleaka said, quickly taking another bite of the sweetened pineapple. "Well done, Anui. You know your plants."

Huko was tired of waiting. "What am I supposed to do with these stupid pieces of pineapple?" he whined.

"Serve your friends," Faleaka told him.

"First of all, they're *not* my friends," Huko said angrily.

"And second, I'm not serving anyone. *I* am supposed to be served. *I* am king," he said, thumping his chest with his hands.

"A very wise man once said, 'A truly great king will find the courage to serve others.'"

"What fool said that?" Huko snarled.

"Your father," Faleaka answered, "and he learned it from the Great King— the One who came to serve all of us."

Huko sat back, shame washing over him. Even though years had passed, he still remembered his father's lessons to him about the Great King and about how all kings should seek to serve their people. But after losing the stone, Huko had feared that his people did not see him as their king, and that they blamed him for his father's death. *I know it is all my fault,* he thought bitterly.

Anui looked at his friend with under-standing in his eyes. He knew Huko's pride and arrogance were just an attempt to hide his fears. But he said nothing.

Faleaka watched the two boys curi-ously, then asked them all, "What has this experience with the pineapples taught you?"

"The importance of using our gifts to turn the ordinary into extraordinary," Allie replied.

"That each of us is significant," Anui answered.

"Excellent. What about you, Billy?" Faleaka asked. "What has it taught you?"

"To never give up," Billy replied, remembering something his mother had once read him from her Bible. "No matter how impossible something might seem."

Faleaka studied Huko but didn't press him for an answer. Then, he added,

"Everything has a purpose and a design—everything *and* everyone."

Allie looked away, tears filling her eyes. *What purpose could I possibly have?* she wondered hopelessly. *My own mother didn't want me.*

Billy thought about his parents' quest for the medallion. In the beginning, it hadn't been just about the medallion, but about giving the people hope again. *Could that be my purpose?* he wondered. *To take back the medallion and free the people?*

Huko still did not speak. He had always believed his purpose was to be king, but the medallion had not worked for him. *What if being king isn't my purpose after all?*

Suddenly, Faleaka cocked his head to one side, listening. "I hear voices," he said.

The kids looked at each other—none of them had heard anything.

"No," Faleaka said, "not in my head, in my ears. We must leave quickly."

## Chapter 19

# The Trackers Are Coming!

At the bottom of the cliff leading up to Faleaka's hut, Kalanu and Makawa were attempting the difficult climb. Makawa, the larger and stronger of the two, climbed quickly, while Kalanu struggled for each new foothold.

Reaching the top, Makawa plucked a mango from a nearby tree and sat down to wait for his partner. Several minutes later, Kalanu heaved himself over the edge and fell flat on the ground, sweating and gasping for breath. He stared up at the munching Makawa with disgust. Staggering to his feet, he began checking for signs that the kids had passed this way, but the rocky ground near the cliff gave no clues.

"Has the great tracker lost them?" Makawa smirked, enjoying his partner's frustration.

"I never lose my quarry," Kalanu said, glaring. "They must have come this way," he muttered to himself.

Then he saw it. A small twig on one of the bushes was twisted and broken in half. Kalanu smiled wickedly. He had them now.

Pushing through the bushes to the clearing, the trackers found Faleaka's hut—and plenty of signs that the two kings and their friends had been there.

"Check the hut," Kalanu whispered, pointing toward the door.

Tiptoeing up to the door, the two men listened for any movement inside, but there was nothing. Kalanu nodded to his partner, and Makawa hurled his body against the door, slamming it open.

Kalanu jumped inside right behind him, but the hut was empty. Kalanu turned to Makawa, crossing his arms over his chest and shaking his head.

"The application of a lesser amount of force would have accomplished the task."

"What does that mean?" Makawa said.

"It means, you could have just *opened* the door!" Kalanu shouted, directing all his frustration at his partner.

"Well, why didn't you just say that?"

Kalanu smacked his forehead. "Oh never mind!" he huffed and began examining the inside of the hut.

"Could it be . . . ?" Kalanu wondered aloud, fingering a smaller, carved version of the statue that stood at the village center. "Yes!" Kalanu shouted. "This is Faleaka's hut! The old man is still alive!"

"How do you know?" asked Makawa.

"Look! This is one of his carvings." Kalanu was now positive the four kids had come to the old man for help. So where were they now? Heading back outside, he saw the bits of pineapple scattered everywhere. Obviously they had done something here. But what?

Watching his partner search for clues, Makawa picked up a piece of Anui's pineapple. Taking a large bite, he had just begun to chew when the terrible taste hit his mouth. Gagging, he spat it out and, turning in circles, looked desperately for something to drink.

His antics drew a questioning look from Kalanu, who picked up the fruit, took a sniff, and tossed it aside.

"Why would anyone desecrate fruit this way?"

"I don't know about *desecrate*, but somebody sure messed up this pineapple," Makawa said, earning himself a smack on the back of the head from his partner.

"Now, where could they have gone?" Kalanu said, resuming his search for clues.

"All your moaning and groaning climbing up the cliff probably scared them away," Makawa jabbed.

Kalanu shot him a dirty look. "Don't be ridiculous."

"Well, they aren't here, are they?" Makawa said, enjoying having the upper hand for a change. "And you cannot find their trail."

"Don't be so certain of that," Kalanu said slowly, as his gaze fastened on a half-eaten mango.

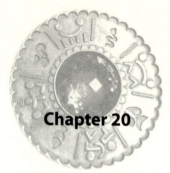

## Chapter 20

# The Great Escape

Faleaka led Billy and the others along the riverbank until they reached a clearing. There he stopped and smiled at them strangely before breaking into a bizarre dance. The kids stared open-mouthed as the old man whirled about, spinning on his toes, leaping, flipping off tree trunks, and even crashing into low-hanging branches—causing them to burst out laughing, but Faleaka silenced them with a finger.

"Now, that will give them something to follow," he said, chuckling softly.

"Give *who* something to follow?" Billy asked.

"Cobra's trackers. They are very near."

"That's why you . . . danced? To cover our tracks?" Huko asked. *Perhaps the old man isn't as crazy as I thought.*

"Yes. Now we must still hurry," Faleaka said.

Continuing along the riverbank, the ground became more and more rocky. A steep cliff rose up along one side, and the path they were on grew narrower. Still they pressed on.

★ ★ ★

Further back, the two trackers were closing in on them. Kalanu might never have found the path Faleaka and the kids had taken if it hadn't been for Anui's unending appetite. The boy had brought along some of the sweetened pineapple when they left the clearing. Munching as he walked, bits of fruit and drops of juice had splattered the ground beneath him, leaving a sticky, sweet trail for Kalanu to follow.

When the trackers arrived at the clearing where Faleaka had performed his dance, Kalanu stopped and looked around in confusion. Makawa scratched his head as his partner suddenly seemed to go insane, leaping and whirling in circles all over the clearing.

"What is wrong with you?" Makawa asked his partner.

"I am following their trail," Kalanu answered.

Makawa thought perhaps his partner had been tracking too long.

Suddenly stopping his mad whirling, Kalanu took a deep breath and pointed, "This way! We must be close now. Signal the others!"

Makawa raised a large conch shell to his lips and blew.

★ ★ ★

The path Faleaka and the kids were on continued to narrow, while the rocky cliff grew higher. Suddenly, they froze as an eerie sound echoed through the jungle, sending a chill up Billy's spine.

*I know that sound,* Billy thought wildly. *Someone is blowing through a conch shell. It must be the trackers. They're closing in on us!*

Looking at Faleaka, Billy could tell he was thinking the same thing.

Starting to panic, they moved as quickly as they could down the ever-narrowing path. Allie led the way, feet slipping and stumbling over loose rocks. Suddenly, she screamed as both the path and the river disappeared, dropping off into a deep gorge, hundreds of feet to the valley below. Her toes hanging over the edge, she flailed her arms backward, trying to regain her balance, but it was too late.

Anui, who had been right behind her, watched in horror as she started to fall. At the last second, Huko ran past him, grabbing Allie's hand and yanking her back to safety. Billy and Faleaka arrived just in time to witness her rescue.

"Allie! Are you all right?" Billy asked, shaken.

"Wow!" Allie exclaimed. "Thanks for saving me."

"You must be more careful, Allie," Anui said, his voice trembling with relief.

Allie took a deep breath. "Now what, Billy?" she asked uneasily.

"What do you mean 'Now what?'" Huko answered instead. "We stay and fight!"

Billy looked around. "We can't fight," he said. "Cobra's men are too well trained. Besides, we don't have any weapons, and there's no place to run."

"We could just stay here and wait for them to throw us off the cliff," Anui said.

But Anui's words planted a crazy idea in Billy's mind. *Crazy, but it just might work!*

"Anui!" Billy exclaimed. "You're brilliant!"

"I am?" Anui asked, puzzled.

Billy started pulling tools from his backpack, handing them out as he spoke. Another blast of the conch shell echoed through the jungle, closer this time.

"Anui, I need some coconuts. Huko, Allie, grab some of those vines," he ordered, pointing to a cluster of long, thick vines hanging down the side of the cliff.

Huko, now too frightened of the approaching trackers, did not bother to argue but quickly set off to get the vines.

While the others had no clue as to what Billy had in mind, Allie thought she knew exactly what he was thinking.

"I could use some help calculating. What do you think, genius?" Billy asked her.

"Nothing like a challenge," she said, hurrying off to gather some vines.

For the first time, the kids worked as a team, while Faleaka stood watch. Everyone knew their job and focused on it—even Huko.

"They are almost here," Faleaka said.

He had barely finished speaking when the trackers appeared at the top of the cliff, a hundred feet above them. Several more of Cobra's warriors had heard the signal and joined them.

Spotting Faleaka and the kids down below, Kalanu shouted, "Get me down there!" as he gestured wildly with a vicious looking machete.

Huko raised Billy's binoculars to his eyes, peering backward through the lens. "They are a long way off," he said.

Allie grabbed the binoculars, turned them around, and gave them back to Huko.

"Oh! Not so far off," he said urgently, watching Cobra's warriors comb the top of the cliff, searching for a way down.

"We have to get down there," they heard Kalanu scream again. "Get me down there!"

Using the vines the others had collected, Billy tied three coconuts to each end of a very long vine. Huko took one end and wrapped it around a large tree, wedging the coconuts into a fork in its branches so that the vine was locked in place.

Billy coiled up the rest of the vine. Then, taking the other end, he swung the coconuts like a lasso, hurling it across the gorge and watching hopefully as it hit the branches of a tree on the other side and wrapped itself around the trunk. Billy gave the vine a tug and the coconuts locked into place.

Above them, Cobra's warriors had found a path down the side of the cliff and were coming fast. Billy and the others were running out of time.

"Almost ready," Billy said, grabbing up another long piece of vine. Using his pocketknife, he sawed it into pieces, each about five feet long. Handing one to each of them, he then slipped on his pack and looped his own piece over the vine that stretched across the gorge. The others copied him. Five pairs of eyes peered over the edge—not sure which was more frightening—Billy's plan or Cobra's warriors.

"We jump on three," Billy said.

"We what?" Faleaka asked, panicking as he realized what Billy planned to do.

"One . . ."

A spear from one of Cobra's warriors flew past, barely missing them.

Billy, deciding it was best to skip number two, shouted, "Three!"

Just as Cobra's warriors reached them, Billy and the others stepped off the side, holding tightly to their vines and zip-lining across the gorge.

"Hold on tight, guys!" Billy screamed.

Arms aching and hearts racing, they held on tight. Within seconds, their feet touched down on the other side of the gorge.

"Ha! Ha!" Faleaka exclaimed with delight and relief. "Let's do that again!"

Huko looked back across the gorge, shaking his head in disbelief. "I can't believe that worked," he said.

★ ★ ★

After cutting down the vine so that the trackers couldn't follow them, the weary travelers continued on, crossing a small stream and waterfall. As Allie stepped up on the bank, Huko graciously turned and offered her his hand to help her up.

"Do you have any royal blood in you?" Huko asked, looking at Allie with interest.

"I . . . I don't know," Allie stammered shyly. "I'm an orphan," she admitted. "But I could do some research . . . at the library."

Huko shook his head at her. "If you were royal, you would know it," he said, dropping her hand.

"I-I could go to the library," Allie said, Huko's words stinging. "They have tons of books there that would have information about . . ."

"You would know," Huko interrupted, dismissing her with a shake of his head.

Allie's temper flared. "You know what? I *do* know this—you're a jerk!"

"No, I'm not," said Huko. "What's a 'jerk'?"

Faleaka, who had stopped to watch, chuckled softly.

"You honestly believe that you're better than us!" Allie accused.

"I am!" Huko insisted, as if this were the most obvious thing in the world. "I am a king."

"That's just a title," Allie shot back. "What's under that skin of yours?"

"Someone very special."

"You don't believe that," said Allie. "Because if you did, you would treat everyone else like they were special too!" she said, brushing past Huko, utterly disgusted with his arrogance.

Huko stared after her. No commoner had ever *dared* to speak to him that way before. But still, he couldn't help wondering, *Could she be right?*

Faleaka chuckled again, catching Huko's eye. "Some of us learn faster than others," he said, turning to follow after Allie.

Huko rolled his eyes. *Crazy old man,* he thought resentfully.

# Chapter 21

# Mohea's Courage

*In the slave camp, on Cobra Island . . .*

Mohea worked as slowly as she dared, trying to delay the completion of Cobra's breastplate. She knew that once it was finished, Cobra would be even more anxious to use the medallion—and she feared not only for her fellow slaves, but also for those still living on Aumakua Island. Spotting the elderly woman she had rescued earlier, Mohea watched her approach, carrying a bucket of water.

Mohea took a long drink, then smiled gratefully.

"Thank you for making them give me lighter work," the old woman said.

"It would be better still if I could get you away from this awful place," Mohea told her. "I must think of some way to free all of us. I hope the water bucket is not too heavy for you."

"Do not worry, my child. It is much lighter than the wood. Besides," she smiled mischievously, "now I can take a nice cool drink whenever I wish, so it is not so bad. As for the other, you will find a way out. I am sure of it."

After the woman moved on, Mohea rested a moment longer. Then, noticing a guard frowning at her, she wiped her sweaty brow with the back of her arm and returned to pounding the metal that would become Cobra's breast-plate. Sparks flew as the heavy hammer struck the red-hot metal.

★ ★ ★

### Inside Cobra's Fortress . . .

Far above Mohea and the other slaves, Cobra called a meeting of his generals and told them his plans.

"Now that the medallion is mine," he said, "I can expand my empire to include all the islands. But the medallion's power has never really been tested. Kieli was a fool. He could have destroyed us with a word. Instead, he chose only to stop our attacks and send us back to this island."

"You should test the medallion to see how powerful the stone really is, my lord," one young general suggested.

"Yes," agreed Cobra. "And my first demonstration will be a perfect test. Tonight, I will destroy Aumakua Island."

The generals looked at each other, stunned. None of them had expected this! But they quickly hid their shock as Cobra narrowed his eyes and scanned each face, looking for objections. Seeing nothing but fear, he smiled.

Only then did one of the generals clear his throat, daring to protest. "My lord," he said bowing low, "I still have warriors on that island."

"They are meaningless to me," Cobra replied coldly, sweeping his hand as if to brush them aside. "They are nothing more than weapons to use as I wish."

The general stared at his unfeeling master but remained quiet. He knew another word could mean his own death. Seeing no further protests, Cobra ordered, "Come!"

After Cobra had strode past them, the younger general whispered, "Destroy the island? He can't do that . . . can he?"

"That is exactly what he will do," the older man replied as he set off after Cobra.

## Chapter 22

# The Test

Later that night, Cobra stood outside his fortress on a terrace overlooking the ocean. He wore robes of a deep, blood red, and the medallion hung from a cord around his neck. Torches flickered in the darkness, casting shadows on the faces of the assembled warriors.

His generals stood silently behind him. Filled with dread, they knew they were not only about to lose several good warriors, but also friends and relatives.

Cobra, eyes glittering with evil, pointed toward Aumakua Island and said in a deep, booming voice, "I ordain my enemies to die!"

But nothing happened. Moments passed, and everyone began to realize that nothing *would* happen.

Puzzled, Cobra stared down at the medallion. *Perhaps I didn't make my wish clear enough,* he thought.

"I wish for that island to . . ." Cobra began.

"Please, my lord!" the older general interrupted, unable to stand it any longer. "Please let me first send for my men," he pleaded.

Frowning, Cobra ignored him, turning away to concentrate on the medallion and the distant island he wanted to destroy. The fate of the general's warriors was unimportant. He could always get more fighting men. But first he needed to test the medallion's power and set an example of what would happen to those who dared defy him.

"I decree for that island to be destroyed by fire from the sky!" Cobra thundered, throwing his clenched hands high into the air.

But again . . . nothing happened. No rumbling. No fire. Not even a streak of lightening.

Lowering his arms to his side, Cobra stared across the waves at the island. Trying once more, Cobra raised his hands, faced Aumakua Island, and shouted, "I wish for that island to be swallowed by the sea!"

Still . . . nothing.

Cobra turned to the general who had dared to question him and said, "I will destroy the island after your warriors return. Send for them."

"Now!" Cobra shouted when the man did not act quickly enough.

The general signaled one of his warriors and gave him the instructions. As the man ran off, the general turned his attention to his king.

Cobra lifted the medallion from his chest and stared at it. *Why didn't it work?* He knew it was powerful. King Kieli had used it against him many times before he died.

Enraged, Cobra stepped up to the general who had dared to plead for his men. Seizing the unfortunate man around the neck, he buried his fang-like nails into his throat.

"This is your fault," Cobra said, coldly watching him die. Dropping the general to the ground, he whirled around and stormed back into his fortress.

## Chapter 23

# Riddles and Failures

*On Aumakua Island...*

Completely unaware of Cobra's attempts to destroy Aumakua Island, Faleaka, Billy, and the others walked on in the darkness, the stars twinkling above them. They had reached the beach and were now following its sandy shoreline. Only Faleaka seemed to know where they were going.

"How are we going to get the medallion back?" Billy asked, hopelessness creeping into his voice.

"Stop!" Faleaka said, holding up his hand and turning to face them all. "Answer this and you will know how to defeat the Cobra."

Seeing that he had their attention, Faleaka continued, *"It is never seen, but always felt. It is sometimes cold, but sometimes melts. A treasure valued more than gold, by poor and rich, by young and old. Strength and power found inside, where worth and purpose both reside."*

The kids looked at him blankly.

"Come!" Faleaka said, motioning for the kids to follow him.

"Could it be the weather?" Huko guessed.

"I don't think that's it," Billy said thoughtfully. Faleaka's words were somehow familiar, but he couldn't quite remember where he had heard them. They sounded like something his mom would have said . . . something about treasures greater than gold.

"Where could power be found?" Allie wondered.

"And what could be more valuable than gold?" Huko asked impatiently. He was angry. Instead of an answer, they had been given yet another riddle.

Noticing that Faleaka had left them far behind, they ran to catch him—each still trying to figure out the answer.

★ ★ ★

### In Cobra's bedchamber . . .

Cobra burst through the door of his bedchamber. Ripping the medallion from around his neck, he flung it across the room. The medallion hit the wall with a loud *CLINK!* and the blue stone popped out, rolling across the floor and into a corner.

"No!" Cobra cried, his anger changing instantly to panic.

Dropping to his knees, he scrambled across the floor to retrieve first the medallion and then the stone. But before he could place the stone back in the medallion, it soared out of his hand and into the air. Hovering for a split second, the stone glowed eerily before sealing itself back in the medallion.

Cobra reverently lifted the medallion over his head.

"Advisor!" he roared, getting to his feet. "I want my advisor!"

Cobra's advisor, a tall, anxious-looking man, came running into the room.

"Why won't the medallion work for me?" Cobra demanded.

The advisor hesitated . . . word had already reached him of the general's death. The rage in his master's voice terrified him. He knew the wrong answer would mean his own death.

"Why?" Cobra shouted.

"The moon," he said shakily, "it is not yet full."

"I do not believe you," Cobra said, eyeing him closely. Too many times he had witnessed Kieli wielding the medallion's power when the sun was high and the moon nowhere in sight.

The advisor searched his mind for something to say and then tried again. "It . . . it needs to rest squarely on your chest," he said, not daring to meet Cobra's gaze. Cobra stepped closer. Softening his voice, he said, "Tell me the truth, and I will do you no harm."

The advisor swallowed hard. Rising fear made him sick to his stomach. He didn't believe Cobra, but he knew he must answer. Lifting his eyes to meet Cobra's, he took a deep breath and said, "The medallion only works for a kind heart."

"Are you saying that my heart is not kind?" Cobra asked quietly, his voice full of venom.

Without warning, Cobra struck, his hand seizing the advisor by the throat. Staring straight into the man's eyes, he lifted his fang-like finger and then plunged it into the man's neck. He held on until the man's body became limp. Then he dropped it to the floor like garbage.

"Not *kind?*" Cobra sneered down at the lifeless body. "Why would you say a thing like that?"

Cobra turned back to the table that sat near his bed and the small bowl of poison that sat upon it. Dipping his fingernail into it, the poison hissed and sizzled, as he shouted, "Bring me a new advisor!"

Then, stepping over to his painting, Cobra dipped a paintbrush in bright red paint. He used it to slash at the work he had so carefully created, leaving the picture spoiled and bleeding. As he slashed, he thought about new ways to destroy the residents of Aumakua Island.

## Chapter 24

# Thieves!

*On Aumakua Island . . .*

Rounding a rocky point, Faleaka and the others heard laughter. Crouching low behind some rocks, they peered out toward the sound. The moon, almost full, lit up the beach and the dozen or so enemy warriors sitting around a campfire.

Disgusted, Huko said, "You old fool! You've led us right to Cobra's warriors."

"Yes . . . and to their boats," Faleaka added sagely.

Three sturdy canoes were beached just a few hundred feet away. A single warrior walked along the water's edge, patrolling the area.

Keeping low to the ground, the five companions left the rocks and crossed the sand to the boats, dropping down behind a large piece of driftwood that lay close to one of the boats.

Faleaka and the kids waited until the guard headed back down the beach, his back to them. Then, moving as quietly as possible, Huko and Billy tried to ease the nearest boat into the water. The vessel creaked but didn't move. Leaning into it, Anui, Allie, and Faleaka added their strength, pushing as hard as they could, but the canoe still would not budge.

"One more time," Billy whispered.

As the five pushed and strained, the boat suddenly lurched over to one side, causing the paddles to roll and bang into each other. The sound caught the guard's attention. He turned back and hurried toward the boats. He glanced briefly at his fellow warriors, but they were too engrossed in their own laughter and hadn't heard a thing.

The guard gripped his spear and raised it shoulder high as he moved toward the boats. As he stopped closer, a large cloud drifted in front of the moon, blocking most of its light and deepening the shadows where Faleaka and the kids hid behind the canoe.

Half-blinded by the darkness, the guard thrust his spear into the shadowy areas in and around the first canoe. Finding nothing, he turned his attention to the second canoe, jabbing here and there. The guard crept still closer, certain he would find the intruder near the last boat. His muscles tensed as he prepared to strike. Raising his spear higher, he aimed it into the darkness of the shadows—and right for Allie's head! She froze, locked in place, unable to move or scream.

But just as he was about to strike, a loud burst of laughter from the warriors around the fire startled him.

"What are you doing?" they called to him. "Fighting shadows?"

Feeling slightly foolish, the warrior cast one last glance toward the boats before heading back to the fire.

Billy forced himself to count to twenty before slowly raising his head up. The way was clear, so he signaled to the others and they crawled from their hiding place.

"Let's try one of the other boats," Anui suggested quietly.

"Good idea," Billy agreed.

Silently, they moved to the next boat in line. Surrounding it, they leaned into the sturdy craft and pushed, sliding it easily into the water.

"Wait," Faleaka cautioned, holding up a hand to halt the others.

 "At times such as this," he whispered, "when great danger must be faced, Huko's father would always remind us of the words of the Great King, 'Be strong. Be courageous. Do not be afraid because the Lord will be with us wherever we go.'"

★ ★ ★

Anui nodded at Faleaka, understanding what they must face. Huko, at the mention of his father, hoped that he did not further dishonor him. And while Allie stared sadly out over the waves, Billy thought of his mother and the many times he had heard her sing those very words.

They each knew that there was no turning back now.

Without the medallion, they had no way to beat Cobra—
and no way for Billy and Allie to return home or to rescue
Billy's dad.

Billy looked at the others and nodded. It was time to
strike back.

**Chapter 25**

# Crossing the Water

Faleaka, Allie, Anui, and Huko scrambled into the boat. But instead of joining them, Billy waded back through the shallow water toward the other two canoes.

"What are you doing?" Allie hissed. "Come on! Let's get out of here."

"Just a second," Billy whispered, motioning for them to wait.

"Get in the boat!" Huko ordered.

But Billy kept going. The others watched as he climbed into one of the remaining boats and knelt down in the bottom. Raising his arm high in the air, he brought it down, swift and hard. He repeated this a couple of times, jumped out, and then slipped into the other boat. There, he quickly repeated the process. Wading back out to the boat, he climbed in with his friends. Faleaka, Huko, Billy, and Anui grabbed the paddles and rowed. As they glided into deeper water, the clouds moved away, and in the bright moonlight, one of the guards spotted them.

"Get them!" he shouted, bringing the warriors running to the two remaining canoes.

Four men climbed into each boat and began rowing, their strong, swift strokes quickly eating up the distance.

"Hurry!" Allie screamed.

"Paddle, paddle! Come on!" Huko shouted.

"I'm paddling as fast as I can," said Billy, turning to see the warriors gaining on them.

"Faster, faster!" urged Faleaka, himself pulling the paddle through the water as fast as he could.

Just as it seemed certain that the warriors would catch them, something strange happened. Cobra's men began shouting in alarm and trying to turn their boats back to shore.

Billy and the others watched as the enemy's boats sank lower and lower in the water, soon dipping out of sight and leaving the warriors swimming for land.

"Ha, ha! Good work, Billy!" Faleaka said, blowing a raspberry back at the swimming warriors.

Billy just grinned.

"I thought you were chickening out," Huko admitted.

Billy reached into his vest, pulled out his pocketknife, and said, "Nope! Me and my trusty knife just had a little job to do."

★ ★ ★

Back on the beach, Cobra's trackers came running up, just as the warriors swam to shore.

Seeing the disappearing boat filled with kids, Kalanu shouted at the soggy warriors, "How could you let them escape?"

"Yeah! How could you let them escape?" Makawa echoed.

"Do you know what Cobra will do to us?" Kalanu said in a panic.

"Yeah! Do you know what Cobra will do us?" Makawa echoed again.

Looking at his partner with disgust, Kalanu said, "I am an idiot," and then shook his head as Makawa parroted back, "I am an idiot!"

"That's the first correct thing you've said all day," Kalanu said as he walked away.

Makawa stared after his partner, not fully understanding what had just happened, then he hurried after him.

★ ★ ★

Darkness swallowed the stolen boat and its passengers as it glided across the ocean toward Cobra Island. They were thankful for the distant torches that guided them toward the island. Cobra insisted that fires be kept burning along the beaches to prevent invaders from slipping unseen onto the island and attacking while everyone slept.

As they paddled, they heard drumbeats coming from the island.

"What are they saying?" Billy asked Anui.

"Let's see," Anui listened closely to the steady beats floating across the waves. "Cobra is having a feast tomorrow night . . . everyone is to come . . . " Anui smiled hungrily. "I'll bet the food will be good."

Faleaka shook his head. "No. There is to be a feast tomorrow, but it is to celebrate the coming destruction of the medallion."

"Oh. I was never good at interpreting drums," Anui admitted.

"Cobra is going to destroy the medallion?" Billy repeated. "We've got to stop him!"

"That medallion is our only way home!" Allie wailed.

"This isn't just about the medallion," Faleaka told them. "Do you understand what this struggle is really about?" he asked.

"I only know that my father died protecting the medallion," Huko said.

"I thought it was about getting the medallion and using its power," Billy said.

"In a way, but the medallion's real power," Faleaka said mysteriously, "doesn't come from its stone."

"What do you mean its power doesn't come from the stone?" Billy asked. "If that's true, then where does the power come from?" *If there's another source of power, he thought, maybe we can use that to defeat Cobra.*

"The medallion's power comes from the Source of all power," Faleaka replied. "And that . . . you must discover on your own."

"It's going to be a long crossing," Faleaka said with a yawn. "You should rest."

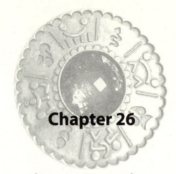

## Chapter 26

# Cobra Island

The sun was just beginning to rise as Billy and the others paddled to shore on Cobra Island. In the distance, they could see part of the fortress, sticking out over the waves like a giant snake's head waiting to strike. Unlike the lush, tropical paradise of Aumakua Island, much of Cobra Island was covered in dark volcanic rock and thick foreboding jungle.

Climbing out, Billy asked, "Where to now?"

"I have a plan," Huko announced. "We will free the slaves and with their help take Cobra's fortress."

"What?" Billy exclaimed.

"We need more people to fight with us, right?" Huko reasoned. "It was *you*, Billy, who said there were only four of us and that we must have help."

"That was before we found Faleaka," Billy argued.

"Now we should be able to get the medallion back, and *after* that we can free the prisoners."

"And I say Faleaka's help is not enough! Look at him! He is an old man who speaks in riddles. We haven't been able to get a straight answer out of him yet. How long do you think he would last against one of Cobra's warriors?" Huko ranted.

"He seemed to do pretty well against you," Billy snapped.

"How long could any of us stand up to Cobra's warriors?" Allie added quietly. "Billy, we're not skilled warriors. Maybe Huko is right."

"Listen to Allie," Huko urged. "If we sneak in at night when everyone is asleep, we can take on the guards and free the others. That will give us a fighting chance to attack Cobra and take back the medallion," Huko said.

"We'll never make it to the slave camp, much less free them! I'm sure they're surrounded by guards," Billy argued, raising his voice.

"I am king, and that is the plan," Huko shouted.

"You don't have a clue and that is a fact," Billy shouted back even louder.

Faleaka stepped between them. "Quiet! You will get us captured with your arguing. Then there will be no one to get the medallion *or* free the prisoners."

But it was too late. High on a ridge above them, one of Cobra's warriors had heard the arguing and moved closer to investigate. Looking down, he spotted the five invaders and took off, sprinting up the hill.

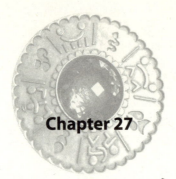

# Chapter 27

# Not an Accident

Huko was tired of Billy's constant interference. "We should get off this beach before someone sees us," he said.

For once, everyone agreed. Spotting a trail, Huko took the lead. Anui and Allie followed, but as Faleaka moved to join them, Billy grabbed his arm, holding him back.

"So what *is* the secret of the medallion's power?" he asked

"Finding that answer is what this journey is all about," Faleaka replied vaguely.

"Why don't you just tell me?"

"If I simply *tell* you what you want to know, you will not learn anything, and the knowledge could easily be lost. But if I make you *seek* the answers, you will better understand them and remember

them. Huko must learn what it means to be a king, and as his descendant, so must you."

"Why? Cobra's descendent Cobb runs the island," Billy explained. "Why would I want to be king anyway?"

"Because you *are* a king with the blood of kings inside you," Faleaka said, gently poking at Billy's heart. "And remember, every person has value—whether he wears a crown or not. This is a truth that Huko has yet to learn."

"I don't understand. You're speaking in riddles again."

"Perhaps, but in time you will understand these truths. Come now, we are falling behind."

Faleaka and Billy hurried to catch up with the others. Making their way inland, they followed a steep path that wound through thick stands of trees. Mangrove trunks twisted together and angled toward the sky. Giant tree roots curled along the ground, waiting to trip the unwary traveler. Even in the morning sunlight, the island felt dark and dangerous, reminding Billy of a haunted forest.

"Ugh!" Allie yelped, dodging a hairy, black spider hanging in its web. "This place is awful!"

Billy followed Huko, scanning the landscape and looking for clues. Farther down the path, they came to an area that seemed familiar to Billy. Giant slabs of blackened, volcanic rock stood amongst the trees. With a start, Billy realized where he was. Rushing past the others, he tackled Huko from behind. Rolling over, the boys struggled briefly before Huko pinned Billy to the ground.

"What are you doing?" Huko demanded.

"Saving your life," Billy responded, pushing the older boy off and sitting up.

Curious, Huko stood as Billy scrambled to his feet. As the others came running up, Billy raised a hand to stop them.

"Watch this," he told Huko. Walking just a few steps farther, Billy stopped and looked around. Spotting a good-sized broken tree branch, he picked it up and tossed it on the ground between two of the stone slabs. The ground sank slightly, then . . . *THWIP! THWIP!* Two deadly bone darts shot out of one of the stone slabs—right at the spot where Huko would have been walking! They hissed across the path and lodged in the tree on the other side of the path.

"My mom showed this to me when I was little," Billy told his stunned audience.

"You should lead," Huko said, stepping back with the others.

The group, with Billy now in the lead, followed the path as it wound up the hill. By now Faleaka had fallen behind. All the climbing was taking a toll on his aging body. Needing to rest, he sat down on a large, smooth boulder to catch his breath.

Seeing Faleaka stop, Allie called to the others, "Hey, guys!" but they were too far ahead to hear her, so she drifted back and sat down with Faleaka.

"Thank you, Allie," he smiled, "for waiting up for an old man."

Allie smiled. "These last few years have been lonely, haven't they?" she asked.

"Yes," Faleaka agreed.

"Then why did you stay in hiding?"

"Why does anyone hide?"

Allie thought for a moment and said, "So they can't be hurt again."

"My job was to protect the king and the people, but I failed. So after the king died, I felt unneeded . . . and unwanted," Faleaka told her.

"I know that feeling," Allie replied sadly.

"Tell me about your family," Faleaka said gently.

"It's not much of a family," Allie admitted, tears stinging her eyes. "My mom told me every day of my life that I was an accident . . . before she left me . . . at the orphanage."

Faleaka looked at her, his face filled with kindness and understanding. "Allie," he said gently, "you may have been an accident to your mother, but you were no accident to God. He created you . . . full of purpose and meaning."

"I want to believe you," Allie whispered, the tiniest glimmer of hope creeping into her heart. "I really do, but . . ."

"It is true, Allie. You just have to believe and trust Him to show you the way."

Allie's eyes sparkled with unshed tears as she considered Faleaka's words.

★ ★ ★

Further ahead, Huko thought he saw movement out of the corner of his eye. He raised his hand, calling to the others to stop.

"What's wrong?" Anui asked.

"I heard something," Huko replied.

The boys strained their ears for any sound but heard nothing.

"I don't hear anything," Billy said. "It was probably an animal or a bird."

"Yes, that must be it," Huko said doubtfully, though he hadn't seen anything living—except spiders—since they'd landed on the island.

They had only gone a little farther, when Cobra's warriors attacked. The boys ran, Huko sprinting ahead of the others. Anui tripped on a tree root, falling face first into the dirt. Huko kept running, but Billy turned back to help him up, giving the warriors time to close in.

"Anui, come on!" Billy urged, pulling him up the path.

Suddenly two warriors burst out of the trees in front of Huko, just as the others caught up. The boys were surrounded. Billy held the staff up like a weapon, ready to fight, but he quickly dropped everything when he found himself facing four deadly spears.

★ ★ ★

Back down the trail, Faleaka tilted his head, listening carefully.

"The boys are in trouble," he whispered.

"We've got to help them," Allie said, starting up the path, but Faleaka grabbed her arm, stopping her.

"No, there are too many of them," he cautioned.

"But if we don't help, they'll be captured and taken to Cobra. We *have* to help," Allie pleaded.

"We can do nothing for them now, Allie. If we expose ourselves to the warriors, we would only be captured too. If we hide, perhaps we can help them later," Faleaka insisted.

Allie searched the old man's face. Had Huko been right when he accused Faleaka of being a coward? Was that the real reason he didn't want to fight the warriors? Faleaka was wise, but if he were unwilling to fight, what chance did they have of defeating Cobra?

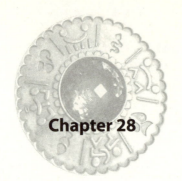

# Chapter 28

# A Tiger's Courage

Knowing the warriors might hunt for them, too, Faleaka pulled Allie behind a large outcropping of rock. Crouching down to wait, they watched as Cobra's warriors ran straight toward them, stopping right in front of their hiding place.

Allie's eyes grew large with fear, but Faleaka pressed a finger to his lips.

"Where are the other two?" one warrior asked the other.

"I don't see them. Are you sure that five came ashore?"

"Yes, but one was an old man and the other a girl. Maybe they stayed behind to guard the boat."

"You're probably right. Let's get back to the others."

The men jogged back to where the boys were being held.

"Put them in the cage," the lead warrior ordered, pointing to a large, bamboo cage that currently held three goats.

The warriors released the goats and forced Billy, Huko, and Anui inside the cage.

The cage was small, so that the boys were forced to crouch on their hands and knees.

"Take them to the slave camp," the lead warrior ordered.

Six warriors threaded long poles through the top of the cage and used them to hoist the cage onto their shoulders. Then they set off toward Cobra's fortress with the other warriors following behind.

★ ★ ★

Faleaka and Allie waited until all the warriors were gone before stepping out of their hiding place. Heading toward the spot where the boys had been captured, Allie spotted Billy's pack. It was lying in the dirt, his stuff spilled across the path. His staff lay nearby. A single tear rolled down Allie's face as she quickly gathered Billy's things and shoved them back inside the pack.

"They are not dead, so there is hope," Faleaka said, his hand patting Allie's arm. "Now is the time for a tiger's courage."

Allie nodded shakily, unable to speak.

"Okay," Faleaka said. "We go find them. Come." Faleaka pointed down the path that the warriors had taken just a short time before.

★ ★ ★

Carrying the heavy cage became even more difficult for the warriors when Huko and Billy began to shove each other, trying to find a comfortable position in their narrow space. One of the men poked them both with his spear.

"You there, settle down," he warned.

"This is humiliating," Huko groaned.

"Yeah? Well, now you know how it feels to bow," Billy shot back at him.

"If we don't get out of here," Billy whispered, "we're gonna end up as prisoners along with the other slaves. Then it'll be impossible to get the medallion back."

"Any suggestions?" Huko asked smartly.

"Yeah, I have an idea," said Billy.

Billy waited until the warriors stopped to rest. They set the heavy cage down in the middle of the path and then moved off to a clearing to rest. Keeping one eye on the warriors, Billy pulled his pocketknife from his vest pocket. Twisting around to see what Billy was doing, Huko spotted the small knife and snorted, "Are you planning to fight Cobra's warriors with that?"

"Did I say I was going to use it as a weapon?" Billy retorted, tired of Huko's complaining.

Checking once more to be sure the warriors were not watching, Billy began to saw at the vines holding the bamboo bars together. While Huko and Anui kept watch, Billy cut through one strip after another along one side of the cage. As he worked, a couple of the poles shifted. Huko grabbed them so they wouldn't fall and alert the guards. Curious, one of the warriors strolled over and peered in at them.

Billy quickly hid the knife behind his back. Seeing

nothing suspicious, the warrior headed back to join the others.

"Okay," Billy whispered. "On the count of three, we'll throw our weight against the side and bust out of here."

"One . . . two . . ." he whispered.

Huko checked to make certain the warriors weren't paying attention, and then nodded to Billy.

"Three!"

All three boys heaved themselves against the weakened side of the cage, breaking the rest of the bindings and forcing the bars to give way. They tumbled to the ground, struggling to rise on legs cramped from crouching so long. But they had no sooner gotten to their feet than they found several spears thrust in their faces. Defeated, the boys sat down on the ground.

The cage was quickly repaired, and the prisoners shoved back inside. The warriors lifted the cage and started toward Cobra's fortress once more.

★ ★ ★

Faleaka and Allie caught up with the boys. Seeing them in the cage, Faleaka leaned over to Allie and asked, "What should we do now, smart one?"

Allie looked at him hopelessly and shrugged her shoulders. "I don't know . . . hide, maybe."

"Remember, Allie," Faleaka encouraged, "like a tiger, not a kitty cat."

"Okay," Allie nodded, shaking herself and trying to think. Fingering the strap on Billy's pack, she suddenly knew exactly what to do! Whispering excitedly, she explained her plan to Faleaka.

★ ★ ★

The next time the warriors stopped to rest, Allie and Faleaka were ready.

Without warning, Faleaka jumped out in front of the warriors, squawking like a deranged chicken and flapping his arms wildly. Two of the warriors chased after the old man, while the others stayed behind to guard the prisoners.

While half the warriors ran after Faleaka, Allie lit a pack of firecrackers she'd found in Billy's pack and threw it at the feet of the remaining warriors. They exploded with machine-gun-like cracks, scattering the frightened warriors, who'd never seen anything like that before. In the midst of the chaos, Allie ran up to the cage and began working at the knot holding the door closed. As she wrestled with it, one of the warriors returned and tried to sneak up behind her.

"Allie!" the boys yelled. "Behind you!"

Instinctively, Allie ducked, crawling between the warrior's legs. Standing up behind him, she kicked him as hard as she could, sending his head crashing into the edge of the cage. While the warrior sat stunned, Allie spun around, landing a perfect roundhouse kick to his temple and knocking him unconscious.

"I can't believe that worked!" she cried. Kneeling down again to work at the knot, she muttered excitedly, "I mean, I've read about how to do that in books, but I never thought it would really work . . . or that *I* could do it!"

Finally loosening the knot, she pulled open the door and the boys scrambled out.

"Come on! Let's go!" she urged them, pointing toward the trees. "Hurry! This way!"

As the kids escaped, the two warriors caught up to Faleaka.

Cowering in fear, Faleaka begged, "Please, I'm a helpless old man. Don't hurt me."

One of the warriors smirked and walked up to Faleaka. Intending to teach the old man a lesson, he swung out with his fist. But Faleaka ducked, spun around, and with a powerful strike to the man's face, dropped the warrior to the ground, unconscious.

Faleaka then turned to the other warrior, once again squawking wildly. Enraged, the warrior rushed toward Faleaka, but a powerful jab left him dazed on the ground as well.

Satisfied, Faleaka dusted off his hands, picked up his own staff, and went to catch up to the others.

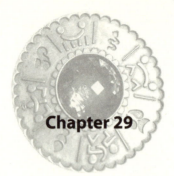

# Chapter 29

# A Wise Man's Sacrifice

Struggling through dense jungle foliage for what seemed like hours, the five weary travelers finally stumbled out onto the beach of a small cove. Emerald green water sparkled in the sunlight. Sheltered on both sides by high cliffs, this part of the island was very different from anything they had seen thus far. It was breathtaking!

While Allie, Huko, and Anui rushed toward the water to cool their aching feet, Faleaka pulled Billy aside.

"I have been watching you for a while now," he said, "and your strengths are easy to see."

Billy shook his head. "My father never saw them."

"He did," Faleaka said knowingly, "but he may have let himself become too busy with other things to tell you."

"I thought that when I found the medallion," Billy said, "then I would find meaning too."

"Billy, you must understand that sometimes the treasure you are seeking is already inside you," Faleaka said, putting his hand over Billy's heart.

Billy nodded slowly, trying to understand.

Faleaka watched him closely, then said, "It's all right. You will understand when the time is right.

★ ★ ★

Unseen by any of them, one of Cobra's warriors stood hidden in the trees just beyond the beach. He patrolled this area regularly and had heard the kids laughing and playing in the surf. Edging forward to investigate, he watched the old man and the boy talking. Taking in the boy's strange dress, he knew that this must be the new king he had heard the others speak of.

*Cobra will reward me richly, if I bring him the body of this strange king,* he thought.

Loading his bow, he pulled back the arrow and patiently waited for a clear shot. When the old man finally stepped away from the boy, the warrior took his shot.

Faleaka's ears were old, but still very sharp. He heard the *thwang!* of the bowstring and the deadly *swoosh!* of the arrow. In a split second, he saw the warrior, still holding his bow. Faleaka threw himself in front of Billy, and the arrow struck him in the chest.

Faleaka fell backward, grabbing his chest. Billy caught him and eased him to the ground. Hearing Faleaka's cry, Huko, Allie, and Anui came running.

Looking up, Billy spotted their attacker, who was already reloading his bow for another shot. Moving quickly, Billy pulled out his sling and pegged the warrior in the forehead with a large stone, knocking him unconscious. Knowing the man would stay that way for a while, the kids gathered around their fallen friend.

Billy gently placed Faleaka's head in his lap. Sensing the boy's distress, the old man reached up and touched Billy's face.

"Why would you die for me?" Billy asked.

"Because the Great King once died for me," Faleaka gasped.

Billy closed his eyes. In his mind, he saw his mother, sitting on her bed and reading to him from her Bible about the Great King. He could still see the light in her eyes as she talked about Jesus, the One who had died to save all mankind. No matter how sick she had gotten, that light had never left her eyes.

Faleaka looked over at Huko, who also knelt beside him, and whispered, "Even though you did not see me, I have watched over you since your father's death. When I see Kieli in the next life, I will tell him of the king you are becoming," Faleaka said, his words fading, as his hand fell back to his chest. Drawing in one last, long breath, he exhaled slowly and was gone.

Tears streaming down his face, Huko closed the old man's eyes. *What could Faleaka say to my father about me?* Huko thought. *That I am arrogant? That I have failed my people by losing the medallion again? How can I make things different?* Silent sobs shook Huko as he thought about the king his father would have wanted him to be.

The four stared at each other, knowing that not only had they lost a wise friend, but also that they were now alone . . . on Cobra Island.

## Chapter 30

# To the Caves

Huko, Anui, Billy, and Allie moved Faleaka's body away from the beach to an area sheltered by trees. There was no time to dig a proper grave, so they carefully wrapped his body in banana leaves and covered him with heavy stones. As Huko set the last stone in place, they each bowed their heads in sadness.

"We should say something," Allie suggested.

"After we recover the medallion and free the slaves, we will take you home to Aumakua Island," Huko said. "You will be honored as a hero."

"Rest in peace, Faleaka. I hope you do see your friend King Kieli again," Allie added.

"Sleep well, friend," Anui said.

"We'll miss your wisdom," Billy finished.

Wiping their eyes, the four friends trudged back to the beach. They had left Cobra's warrior gagged and tied to a tree.

"So now what do we do?" Anui asked.

Billy thought for a moment and said, "We work together as one. And we carry out what I think was Faleaka's plan."

Huko nodded silently. He was beginning to see that escaping Cobra Island—with the medallion and his people—would mean they must all work together as one.

"We have to figure out the answer to Faleaka's last riddle. He said that it would tell us how to defeat Cobra," Billy insisted.

"But with Faleaka gone, how will we know if we have the right answer?" Huko said.

Allie tried to change the subject. "What else besides those darts did your parents show you on this island?" she asked.

Billy pulled out his map and studied it. "North of here, farther down the coast, are caves leading into Cobra's fortress," he said, pointing out over the water past the cliffs. "We can sneak into the fortress through the caves and take back the medallion. But we can't get to the caves by land. We have to go by water.

"It's too far to swim," Huko said.

Allie sat down in the sand. Picking up a small piece of driftwood, she threw it into the water and watched it float with the tide.

Suddenly, her eyes lit up. "I have an idea," she said.

★ ★ ★

Inside Cobra's throne room, a huge feast had been prepared.

Cobra stood and addressed his army. "Tomorrow we will destroy that which is weak and worthless! Tonight . . . we feast!"

The warriors cheered and began to chant, "King Cobra! King Cobra!"

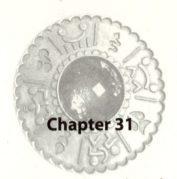

## Chapter 31

# Which Way Did They Go?

It had taken the trackers hours to make their way back to Cobra Island and then to the beach where the kids had been. Once there, they carefully searched the shoreline for clues, finding numerous tracks as well as a trail of blood.

"It would appear that someone was gravely injured here, possibly even killed," Kalanu said as he examined the spot. "Look over there—a body was dragged that way."

Following the trail, the trackers discovered Faleaka's body. They lifted just enough stones from the pile to see who was buried there.

"It's the old man," Makawa said, surprised.

"The warrior who patrols these shores must have spotted the prisoners and tried to stop them."

"Then where are they now? And where is the warrior?" Makawa wondered.

"Let's go back and examine the beach again."

"Good idea."

Before long the trackers located the bound and gagged warrior. Kalanu used his knife to cut the vines and free the man.

"What happened?" he asked the warrior.

"That new king tricked me," the angry man said, pointing to a large bruise on his forehead. "Pulled out some sort of contraption and hit me with a stone."

"You let yourself be captured by children?" Makawa laughed, thinking that even he wasn't that dumb.

"I was knocked out!" the warrior shouted. "When I awoke, I was tied to this tree."

"So where are the kids now?" Kalanu asked.

"All the tracks end at the edge of the water," Makawa added.

"Wait!" Kalani yelled excitedly. "That's it!" He searched the beach until he came to a cluster of driftwood. "Several large pieces of wood are missing from this spot," he said. "See the indentations?"

"It looks like they dragged the wood toward the water," Makawa said. "But why would they do that?"

"Because that is where they escaped," Kalanu proclaimed, "through the water!"

"But which way did they go?" Makawa asked.

"That I do not know," Kalanu admitted.

"Then we have lost them," Makala said, dejected. "When Cobra finds out, we are doomed."

"No! We'll keep searching. There's no need to tell Cobra yet," Kalanu said. "The question is why did they come to Cobra Island in the first place?" Kalanu asked.

"Maybe they wanted to rescue the prisoners from the slave camp," Makawa answered.

"What would that accomplish? Cobra's warriors would simply replace the slaves with others. No, I think the young ones had a more devious plot in mind."

"Like what?"

"Like retrieving the medallion."

"Not possible," Makawa said.

"Think about it," said Kalanu. "If you were the rightful king and wanted to set your people free from someone as powerful as Cobra, what would you do?"

Makawa thought a moment, and then his face lit up. "I would try to get the one thing that would give me a chance to win."

"Indubitably."

"In due be what?"

"It means 'of course,'" Kalanu explained with a sigh. Then he sat down on a piece of driftwood and tried to figure out which way the kids might have gone.

## Chapter 32

# Hanging Around

Seizing upon Allie's idea, the four kids had each grabbed a large, smooth piece of driftwood. Holding on, they had used them as floats to paddle around the cliff, down the coast, and right up to the entrance of the caves.

Entering the caves, Billy and the others looked anxiously at the wet, rocky sides.

"We don't want to be in these caves during high tide," Allie said. "From the looks of this water line, I'll bet they flood every day."

Spotting a pile of torches placed high up on one of the rock ledges, Billy climbed up and handed down a couple. Lighting them, they moved farther into the caves. Since he had been inside these caves with his father, Billy led the way, with Huko bringing up the rear.

"Where does this go?" Huko asked.

"To Cobra's throne room, I think," Billy replied.

As they went deeper into the tunnel, the ceiling grew steadily lower, so that they had to bend low to avoid bumping their heads. But after just a few more feet, the ceiling disappeared, rising high above them as the tunnel opened into an underground grotto. Several other tunnels branched off of it. One path was clearly marked with torches, making Billy wonder if it were also patrolled. *I hope we don't run into any of Cobra's warriors down here,* he thought. *There's not too many places to hide.*

Following the torches, Billy pressed on, the others following close behind, until they reached a large opening that looked out over Cobra's throne room. Inching their way up to the opening, they slowly peered over the edge, just enough to see what was happening in the room below.

The celebration was apparently over. Sleeping warriors lay everywhere, on benches and under tables and sprawled out on the floor. Passed out from too much food and excitement, they were deaf to anything happening in the hall. Even Cobra had not sought his bed that night and had instead fallen asleep on his throne.

Thanks to the many torches that had been left burning, Billy was able to see clearly. He looked down at the throne, which was located directly below him. Motioning for the others to join him, Billy waited while they crawled up next to him. Then he pointed wordlessly to the medallion on Cobra's chest.

Moving as quietly as possible, Billy pulled a compact fishing pole from his pack, wincing at the noise as he snapped the sections together. Peeking over the edge, he was relieved to see that Cobra and his men were still sleeping soundly.

Billy then flicked the release lever, silently lowering the hook. Holding his breath, he carefully guided the hook to its target.

"Left . . . more to the left," Allie whispered nervously as she leaned out to watch.

The hook clinked softly when it landed on the medallion. Billy guided the hook toward the knot at the top of the medallion, trying to snag the cord. But the hook slipped, brushing Cobra's cheek and causing the man to snort loudly and swat at it as Billy quickly yanked the line out of reach.

Heart pounding, Billy began again, guiding the hook carefully. With a flick of his wrist he twisted the line, causing the hook to flip over and catch in the knot. His eyes lit up. *Yes,* he thought in triumph as began to reel it in. The necklace rose slowly, rotating slightly as it dangled at the end of the line.

Suddenly Cobra shifted, whacking the medallion and knocking it off the hook, so that it fell back to his chest. Not daring to even breathe, Billy waited to see if Cobra would awaken. But he did not.

Billy sighed. Clearly, this was not working. Pulling up his hook, he broke down the fishing rod and packed it away. Thinking for a moment, he then signaled the others to head back inside the cave.

"I have another idea," Billy said. "Huko, Anui, go back and get those vines we saw on the walls. Remember?"

The boys nodded and hurried away.

When they returned, Billy handed Huko one end of the vine.

"I need you to hold this for me," Billy told him.

Huko, figuring out what Billy was up to, shook his head. "I do not think this is a good idea," he said.

"Well, neither do I," admitted Billy. "But do you have a better one?"

Huko shook his head and took the vine.

The four then made their way back to the opening above the throne. It was just large enough for all four kids to lie side by side. Once in position, Allie and Anui braced Huko as he lowered the vine over the edge.

The room was silent except for the occasional loud snore. Grabbing the vine, Billy lowered himself over the edge while Huko, Allie, and Anui held on tightly. Slowly, Billy worked his way down the wall behind the throne, holding tightly to the vine. Dangling just above Cobra's head, Billy held the vine with one hand and reached for the medallion with the other, sweat beading on his forehead. But just as his fingers lifted up the cord, Cobra turned in his sleep, pulling it from his grasp. Billy reached down to try again. At that same moment, one of the sleeping warriors rolled over, accidentally elbowing the man sleeping next to him in the head.

Billy froze, not daring to move. The man groaned loudly and rubbed his injured head. He started to sit up, but then just rolled over and went back to sleep. All four kids sighed with relief as the man's snores rejoined the others. Unfortunately, the incident had made Billy's hands so sweaty that this time, as he reached for the medallion, he lost his grip on the vine and fell—right toward Cobra!

## Chapter 33

# Facing the Enemy

Allie's hand flew to her mouth, stifling a scream. But as he fell, Billy managed to reach out with both hands and grab the vine. Though his hands continued to slide, he was able to control his fall. At the last second he let go, spreading his legs and landing perfectly on the massive arms of the throne. Billy watched Cobra fearfully, waiting to see if he would awaken. But he did not.

Knowing he had to act fast, Billy climbed down off the throne. Leaning over his enemy, he reached out once again to get the medallion. Before he could lift it, Cobra turned again, so that he was facing Billy, his rancid breath ruffling Billy's hair. Billy glanced up at his friends, his mouth twisted in disgust.

★ ★ ★

In the hallway outside, a guard patrolled his regular route. He was headed toward the throne room, but along the way, he opened every door he passed, checking the rooms. Cobra was very strict when it came to security, and his guards were commanded to check every area and passage they passed. Even though the guard knew that Cobra was surrounded by his finest warriors, he would still follow orders.

As the guard made his way toward the throne room, his footsteps echoed in the quiet hallway, but Billy was concentrating too hard on the medallion to hear them. Leaning over, he lifted the medallion while the guard checked the room next door. Finding it empty, the guard crossed over and checked the room across the hall as Billy lifted the medallion higher.

With the medallion now at eye level, Billy leaned over even farther to pass the medallion over Cobra's head without waking him. He was barely two inches from Cobra's face when the guard crossed the hall and reached for the massive, cobra-shaped handles on the throne room doors. Trying not to awaken anyone, he slowly eased one door open, but it still creaked loudly.

Billy's head shot up at the sound, and seeing the opening door, he carefully laid the medallion back on Cobra's chest.

As the door inched open wider, Billy slipped behind the throne. Huko quickly pulled up the vine, and the three kids backed up into the cave, hoping they couldn't be seen. The guard stepped inside and scanned his eyes over the sleeping men. As he did, he thought he saw movement near the throne.

Worried, he stepped farther into the room, straining his neck to see behind the throne. Billy held his breath. If the guard spotted him, it would be over.

Still unsure if he had seen movement or not, the guard took a few steps forward and nearly stumbled over a sleeping warrior. Trying to cross the floor would be next to impossible without waking someone up. And if that someone were Cobra, the guard knew he could end up being thrown into the Pit of Death. Looking toward the throne once more, he still saw nothing. Shrugging, he left the room, closing the door softly behind him.

Starting to breathe again, Billy crept out from behind the throne and once more lifted the medallion from the chest of the sleeping Cobra. Using both hands this time, Billy lifted the necklace higher, but as he pulled it over his enemy's head, Cobra's eyes suddenly snapped open.

For a split-second, Billy and Cobra stared at one another, neither moving. Then Cobra shouted, "Guards!"

Billy leaped down from the throne's platform to the floor below, yelling up to the others, "Go! Go! I'll meet you where we came in."

Confused and half asleep, Cobra's warriors struggled to their feet, looking for an invading army, but finding none. Billy darted around the room, dodging this way and that, trying to reach the doors. But it was a losing battle.

Looking up, Cobra saw Huko, Allie, and Anui on the ledge. "Get them!" he yelled, pointing at the threesome.

As they disappeared from into the cave, several guards ran out the double doors and headed toward the tunnels.

★ ★ ★

Huko, Allie, and Anui ran back down the tunnel. But in their rush, they took a wrong turn. Running from tunnel to tunnel, they couldn't find the way out. Hearing footsteps behind them, they knew Cobra's warriors were closing in on them. Allie stopped running, bringing both boys to a halt. Placing a finger to her lips, she pointed to her ear, indicating they should listen to find out where the guards were.

Allie pulled the boys back several steps into the shadows. Ahead was yet another cross tunnel, and as they waited, the warriors appeared and headed left into it. When the sound of their footsteps faded, the fugitives ran down the opposite tunnel.

They might yet have escaped the caves, but unfortunately, Anui did not see the trip wire. Stumbling over it, he triggered one of Cobra's many traps. A huge, flat stone studded with bone spikes swung down from the ceiling. As its deadly spikes rushed toward them, Allie, Huko, and Anui screamed in terror.

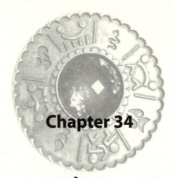

## Chapter 34

# Captured . . . Again!

Inside the throne room, Cobra threatened his men, "If that boy escapes, every one of you will spend the rest of your lives in my slave camp."

Several warriors ran to guard the massive doors, while others lifted a huge wooden beam and lowered it into hand-carved holders, bolting the door. This cut off Billy's only route of escape, but he was too busy dodging other warriors to notice.

Despite his best efforts, Billy was soon surrounded. Realizing his defeat, he stopped running and stood tall, facing Cobra defiantly. As Cobra stepped nearer, Billy brandished his staff at him threateningly.

"Who are *you* to challenge me?" Cobra laughed down at him. "You are nothing but a worm."

"You may have captured me," Billy shouted bravely,

"but the others got away. They'll be back to get the medallion. Wait and see!"

Without warning, Cobra drew his arm back and struck Billy hard across the temple. Billy staggered and then dropped to the floor, unconscious.

"Lock him away in the dungeon," Cobra ordered. "See to it that he does not escape."

"Yes, my lord," his warriors replied as they carried Billy out of the throne room.

★ ★ ★

Cobra returned to his bedchamber. As he entered the room, his new advisor stepped out of the shadows.

"Where is the boy?" he asked Cobra.

"In a cell, in my dungeon," Cobra said without looking up.

"You must make him your friend," the advisor said. With his one good eye, he stared at Cobra. The other eye was covered by a thick, black patch—a souvenir of one of Cobra's many wars.

"He is my enemy," Cobra said viciously.

"But as your friend, he will give you his heart," the advisor said. "As your new advisor, I tell you . . . with his heart, you will gain the world."

Cobra nodded slowly, a plan beginning to form. Earlier, he had received word that the others had fallen victim to one of his traps. Perhaps he could use that information to convince Billy to join him.

*And perhaps,* he thought, *I should not destroy the medallion just yet . . . though the threat of it just might keep this new king in line.*

★ ★ ★

Hours later, Billy began to stir. His brain was still foggy, but he could feel something moving near his feet. Slowly, it moved up his leg. Struggling to stay conscious, Billy managed to lift his head . . . and found himself staring into the cold, dead eyes of a hooded cobra!

Before he could scream a hand reached down and casually plucked the snake off him, dropping it into a woven basket and covering it with a lid. Sitting down across from Billy, Cobra placed the basket next to him.

"Deadly," Cobra said of the snake.

Billy struggled to sit up, but a bout of dizziness overwhelmed him, and he dropped his head into his hands, closing his eyes. Opening them again, he looked around the cell. It was only about nine feet wide and seven feet deep. A hard, flat stone served as his bed. A similar stone bed was on the other side of the cell, and this was where Cobra sat.

Billy noted the thick bars that covered the doorway. The only light came from the torches flickering in the hall, so that he couldn't be sure if it were night or day. Billy tried to remember his father's drawings of the ruins of Cobra's fortress. In his mind's eye, he traveled the massive building, struggling to remember the layout and to figure out some way to escape.

All this, while Cobra stared at him silently, almost . . . kindly. After a moment Cobra asked, "Did you sleep well, my friend?"

Billy eyed him, shaking his head. "I'm not your friend," he said resentfully.

"But you are in need of friends," Cobra answered calmly.

"I already have friends."

"No," Cobra said, leaning closer. "You had friends," his voice dripping with pretended sympathy. "They set off a trap last night as they were trying to escape. They were killed."

Billy heart seemed to stop as the meaning of Cobra's words sank in.

"I'm so sorry," Cobra said. He then rose quietly and, taking the snake, he left the cell, leaving Billy alone with his thoughts.

Stunned, Billy turned his face to the wall to hide his tears. There was no way he was going to let that monster to see him cry.

**Chapter 35**

# A Tempting Offer

Billy could hardly believe the news that Cobra had so cruelly delivered.

"Dead?" he whispered, tears spilling down his cheeks. "First Faleaka, now this? What have I done? This is all my fault."

Heartbroken, Billy mourned the loss of his new friends, but what hurt the most was losing Allie—his best friend. Unable to lie still any longer, Billy stood up and paced the floor of his tiny cell. Passing the cell door, he spotted his pack in the corridor outside his cell, its contents scattered across the floor. He couldn't reach any of his stuff, but the pack was closer. Squatting down, Billy reached out through the bars, straining to reach the strap.

"Come on, come on," he whispered, stretching until his muscles burned. But his fingertips only brushed the edge of the strap. Pulling his arm back inside, Billy looked closely at the bars. Then, twisting slightly, he angled his shoulder to push it partway through the opening. It was a tight fit, but stretching as far as he could, he managed to hook one finger under the strap and pull the pack into the cell. It might be empty, but at least he could use it as a pillow.

Stretching back out on the stone bed, he slipped the pack under his head and thought about Cobra's words. Obviously, the man wanted something from him, but what was it?

After a while, Billy drifted to sleep, but it wasn't long before a noise outside his cell woke him. Sitting up with a start, he found Cobra watching him through the bars.

"Bad dream?" Cobra asked.

"Go away," Billy said in a nasty voice.

Cobra's eyes narrowed, but he held his temper in check. Softening his voice, he said, "You must be hungry. When was the last time you ate?"

Billy's stomach picked that moment to growl loudly, bringing a knowing grin to Cobra's face.

"There is no need for us to be enemies," Cobra told him. "Join me. We will do many great things together."

"What great things would that be?" Billy asked.

"We could unite the islands under one ruler."

"What makes you think the islands would be better under a single ruler—especially you?"

"It would eliminate future . . . conflicts."

"Conflicts?" Billy asked. "You mean like when you killed King Kieli and took over Aumakua Island?"

"I was wrong to have killed him," Cobra said, dropping his eyes in pretended sorrow. "Not a day goes by that I don't wish I had spared his life. I want to be a good king, but I need your help to show me how."

Billy studied Cobra's face. He knew the man was lying, but why?

"Together we can make life good for everyone," Cobra persisted.

"We can't make things good for my friends."

"I am sorry about that. But together we can stop things like that from ever happening again. Your life could matter in so many ways."

"My friends are dead. Nothing matters anymore," Billy said, all hope gone from his voice.

"Oh, but you are wrong, my friend. Join me for dinner, and I will free twenty slaves whether you decide to help me or not. That would matter, would it not?" Cobra asked. "A little cooperation on your part could prevent a lot of suffering."

"How do I know you won't just make them slaves again later?" Billy asked.

"You don't trust me," Cobra said, a hurt expression on his face.

"Why should I? You're the bad guy here."

"So much distrust for a boy your age. What if I give you my word that I will not send my warriors out to capture them again?"

"How do I know your word is any good?"

Losing his patience, Cobra's voice turned threatening. "You dare much, little man."

"What've I got to lose?"

"I could crush you like an annoying little bug," Cobra growled.

Billy bit his lip to keep from smiling. Cobra was beginning to show his true colors. *But why all the pretending?* Billy wondered.

Spotting Billy's expression, Cobra tried a different approach.

"You think you are very clever, do you not? But I assure you, you will be joining me for dinner. If you refuse to dine with me, I will have those same twenty slaves put to death." Cobra gave him one last cold smile before turning to leave.

Billy watched him go, stunned. *If I don't dine with Cobra,* he thought, *twenty innocent people will die!*

Jumping to his feet, Billy grabbed the bars and yelled, "Okay! I'll eat with you!"

Cobra's evil laugh floated back to him for an answer.

# Chapter 36

# Dinner with a Snake

Later that night, Cobra had Billy brought to his dining hall, where he'd had a great feast laid. Billy sat at one end of a large wooden table, while Cobra sat at the other end, surrounded by warriors and slaves who waited to do his bidding.

"What do you want from me? Billy demanded.

"I want you to help me make the medallion work," Cobra admitted.

"You need my heart," Billy said slowly, at last beginning to understand something of what Cobra really wanted.

"Yes," Cobra admitted. "If you help me, then together we can share in the medallion's power." And then, somehow sensing Billy's weakness, he added, "And you will be . . . *special*."

"You can use it for good," Cobra continued, "and I will

use it to rule. We can both get what we want. Who knows, perhaps I might learn from your kindness."

"That's not likely," Billy muttered, gulping down some pineapple juice.

"Your compassion allows you to see things differently," Cobra said, taking a bite of bread. "I've been thinking . . . we would be a perfect balance for each other. I have the strength and power to protect my subjects, while you have the goodness needed to take care of them. You could use the medallion to make sure that no one goes hungry and to heal the sick."

Billy shoveled more food into his mouth to avoid speaking.

"I am not as heartless as some would have you believe," Cobra said.

"Really?" Billy said. "All of the books I read say you're pretty ruthless, and since Allie and I came, you haven't done anything to prove them wrong."

"There are books written about me?" Cobra asked, his interest rising.

"None of them are flattering, but you could change all that."

"With your help, maybe I could," Cobra lied.

The two enemies ate in silence for a bit, eyeing each other.

"Aside from setting the slaves free, what would you do for the people if you could use the medallion?" Cobra asked slyly.

"I don't know," Billy said quietly, thinking of his father.

"So will you join me?" Cobra asked.

Billy hesitated. He knew he couldn't help Cobra, but how could he avoid it without putting the slaves in greater danger?

"Why don't I give you more time to think about it?" Cobra offered, as he signaling one of his warriors to take Billy back to his cell.

# Chapter 37

# Giving Up

Back in his cell, Billy stared blankly at the ceiling for most of the night, his jumbled thoughts refusing to focus on anything. Hours had passed since he had been taken from the dining hall. If his cell had a window, he might have noticed the sun rising. Stretching his aching muscles, Billy stood and began pacing back and forth to ease the soreness.

He had now figured out exactly where he was in Cobra's fortress. His cell was in one of the six prison areas, far below ground. He knew there was at least one staircase leading to the floor above and another leading farther down into the dungeons—probably to where the slaves were kept. Both, he guessed, would be heavily guarded.

*I've got to get out of here,* Billy thought. *But how?*

★ ★ ★

While Billy had been dining with Cobra, Allie, Anui, and Huko had found themselves being shoved into the terrible heat and semi-darkness of the slave camp. Forced to make weapons along with the other slaves, they soon met up with Mohea, who shared her escape plan with them.

"We should go at night when there are fewer guards," Allie suggested.

"Yes," Mohea agreed. "Even those who are on duty will be sleepy and not as watchful."

"What difference does it make how sleepy the guards are?" Huko growled. "Three or four people do not stand a chance against Cobra's might."

"If you'd been paying attention," Allie snapped, her patience gone, "you'd know that once we escape, we can find out if Billy is still alive. If he is, we'll set him free and try to take back the medallion."

"And if he isn't alive? Then what?" Huko asked.

Allie didn't even want to think about that possibility. "He is alive. He has to be," she said stubbornly.

"And what if he's not? If Billy is dead, what good is the medallion if no one can use it?" Huko wanted to know. "You should just forget about escape and accept your new life as a slave."

"But you could use the medallion," Allie said. "You're the true heir."

"It did not work for me, remember?" Huko said.

"It didn't work because it wasn't on your chest," Anui said.

"Bah! What do you know?" Huko muttered as he jumped to his feet and stormed away.

**Chapter 38**

# A New Hope

To keep the guards from becoming suspicious, Mohea, Allie, and Anui went about their work as usual. But as they moved about the camp, they searched out places to hide weapons, in dark crevices of the cave. They also shared their plan with a few of the camp's most trustworthy villagers.

"But where will we go when we escape?" a young father asked. "Now that Cobra has destroyed our island, we no longer have a home."

Allie was horrified. "You mean no one told you?"

"Told us what?" Mohea asked.

"Cobra *tried* to destroy the island, but the medallion didn't work for him. The island is safe."

Relief—and hope—spread through the camp like wild-fire. Mohea and the others decided to try to get weapons for everyone. Though Mohea, Allie, Anui, and Huko would try to slip away first, they wanted the other slaves to be ready to strike when their chance came.

Working carefully, they began sneaking swords and daggers from the stockpiles before they were loaded on the carts to take up to the fortress. They didn't dare take too many at once because the guards might grow suspicious, especially if they thought production were slowing.

As Allie worked, she also worried about Billy. Because he had not shown up at the slave camp, she feared that he really might be dead. Mohea tried to keep Allie's hopes up, but she, too, believed the worst.

As the day wore on, Mohea took a break from forging weapons to get a drink and wipe the sweat from her face. When she did, she saw Huko sitting off to the side, head down, mindlessly shaping an arrowhead. Watching Huko's slow, sullen movements, anger flared inside her as bright and hot as the fiery furnaces. *Enough!* she thought, stamping over to him, hands on hips.

"What are you doing?" Mohea demanded.

Huko refused to look up or answer.

"Answer me!"

"What does it look like?" Huko said. "I'm working."

"You are acting like a spoiled child, moping because you have to do a little work. Grow up, Huko, and act like a man! You should be doing everything you can to escape this place and free your people. You are the king," Mohea scolded him. "Start acting like one!"

"I am a slave," Huko said, sounding defeated.

"*All* kings are slaves," Mohea said. "When my mother carved the mold for your father's medallion, she spent many hours with him, deciding what to engrave in the metal. Your father *served* his people. Huko, I have watched you my entire life. I can see your father in you. It is time you become the man he was!"

Huko was shocked that Mohea would speak to him that way.

*Who does she think she is?* he thought. *She has no right to speak to me with such disrespect—or to tell me what to do. I am a king! She is just a slave!* Then he remembered . . . *just like me.* Slowly, the truth of her words began to sink in.

Mohea narrowed her eyes and said, "Either you start acting like their king, or I'm going to start acting like their queen." Then she added softly, "The people must believe in themselves again . . . and they need you to help them do it."

Having seen Mohea and Huko talking, Allie and Anui had eased closer to them, pretending to work.

Beside them now, Allie said, "Huko, you know we must escape, and to do that the villagers need to have faith in themselves and in you as their rightful king. You can't expect them to find the courage to fight for their freedom when they see you just sitting here like you've given up."

Mohea knelt in front of Huko and took his hands. "I was not lying when I told you that I see your father in you. I know he is here and here," she said, tapping first his chest and then his head. "You have great strength inside you, Huko. I know it. Please," Mohea pleaded, "your people need you."

Huko hung his head. "I'm sorry," he said in a low voice. "Ever since I lost the stone, I have felt so guilty. I know it is my fault my father died that day . . . and my fault our people are slaves."

"It is time to forgive yourself, Huko," Mohea said wisely. "You were just a child, too young to understand the consequences of your actions."

"But can you forgive me?" Huko asked looking from one to the other.

"I forgive you, Huko," Anui said, as Allie and Mohea nodded. "And the people will too."

"They're waiting for you to lead them like your father did," Allie added.

"Show them the king you can become," Mohea said, eyes bright.

"You there! Break it up!" a guard shouted. "Get busy and don't let me see the four of you talking together again!"

But from that moment on, Huko was a new person . . . and his new attitude spread quickly to the others. He and Anui moved about the camp carrying metal, supplies, and hope to the slaves.

★ ★ ★

Billy tossed back and forth on his stone cot, moaning over and over, "Go away . . . leave me alone . . . go away."

Suddenly his eyes snapped open, and he saw Faleaka sitting across from him, smiling. Confused, Billy sat up and looked at him. "Faleaka?"

"Yes, Billy."

"Faleaka," Billy confessed, "I didn't get the medallion."

"It was never about the medallion," Faleaka assured him.

"But everything's gone wrong. We tried to steal the

medallion from Cobra, but I couldn't get it. I was captured and the others . . . they're . . . dead."

"You will have a chance to escape," Faleaka interrupted. "You must be ready. It will be dangerous. There will be many obstacles in your way, but you can overcome them."

"Didn't you hear me?" Billy shouted at him, all his worry and frustration pouring out. "Allie, Huko, and Anui are dead, Faleaka! I failed them! When they tried to escape through the tunnels, they triggered a trap. Even if I do find a way out of here, what am I gonna to do without their help? I can't fight Cobra on my own."

Faleaka did not answer. He looked at Billy, his eyes gentle and understanding.

"I'm never going to get the medallion," Billy went on. "Cobra has it, and there's no way for me to get it back. He is king now."

"A crown does not make a person a king. Just as finding a lost medallion does not make a man an archeologist, or a spear make a warrior," Faleaka said simply.

"I've ruined everything by coming back. Instead of fixing the future, I've just made it worse because now Cobra is going to destroy the medallion," Billy finished in a whisper.

"Billy, this isn't about the medallion or who has it. Medallions don't make us noble. Our value is not determined by what is on the outside. Our value is determined by what is inside," Faleaka said, stretching out his hand and laying it over Billy's heart.

At Faleaka's touch, Billy felt a deep warmth and peace filling him, so he was startled when his heartbeat began to change, becoming a harsh, metallic *CLANG! CLANG!*

Billy awoke with a start, looking all around his cell for Faleaka before realizing it had been a dream. Searching for the source of the clanging, Billy saw Cobra shaking the cell door. At his feet sat a basket . . . which Billy now knew from his previous encounter contained a deadly cobra.

## Chapter 39

# Sentenced to Die

"So . . . will you help me, my friend?" Cobra asked, still trying to be pleasant.

Billy stared at the cage at Faleaka's feet and refused to answer.

"Do not ignore me," Cobra threatened.

Billy stood and faced his enemy. Shaking his head, he said, "No. I will not help you do evil, whether I have the medallion or not."

"Then your death will precede the medallion's destruction," Cobra roared and started to leave, but then he paused.

"I almost forgot," he said, picking up the basket. Kneeling down, he opened it and gave it a slight shake—causing one of the biggest cobras Billy had ever seen to slither into the cell with him.

"Meet your new cellmate. I hope you enjoy each other's company," Cobra said, straightening. "And by the way . . . your friends? They aren't really dead. But they will be—soon—as will you."

Billy stared at the hissing cobra gliding toward him. He leaped up on his stone bed as Cobra walked away, laughing. Reaching into his pocket, Billy pulled out the handful of stones he always kept there. Choosing one, he returned the rest to his pocket. Taking careful aim, he threw it at the snake's head, hitting it squarely between the eyes. The blow sent the serpent reeling backward into a corner.

Keeping one eye on the snake, Billy stared at the lock that was keeping him trapped in here. Then he realized . . . *the lock! That's it,* he thought. *Why didn't I think of it before?*

Peering through the bars, Billy surveyed the contents of his bag strewn across the floor. *It's not there,* his heart sinking. *But if it's not there, then maybe . . . maybe . . .*

Glancing back at the snake, he saw that it was moving toward him again, its head raised, weaving back and forth to strike.

Billy knew he had to escape before the deadly cobra bit him. Digging through his pack, he searched for the ring of lock picks. If it wasn't out there with his other stuff, maybe it was still in the pack. The cobra moved closer, hissing and spitting. Billy jumped over it and across to the other stone bed, taking his pack with him and narrowly avoiding a painful bite as the hooded snake lunged at his leg.

*Where is that pick?* Billy thought desperately.

Thrusting his hand inside, he searched every inch of the pack and its many pockets. Leaping back across the three-foot space to avoid another strike, Billy's frantic thoughts threatened to overwhelm him.

*Where is it? It has to be here somewhere!*

Desperate, he searched the last of the pockets, as he continued to dodge the cobra. *There!* He felt it—the thin, metal ring was wedged in the crease of one of the pockets. Billy sighed with relief as he pulled out the picks.

Jumping back to the bed closest to the lock, Billy set to work, trying to open it. But the lock was very different than the ones he was used to—and the cobra was very angry! Its body weaved back and forth, hissing and spitting, waiting for a chance to strike and making Billy's job even more difficult. He had to stop often to swat back the snake with his pack.

Then, his fingers slippery with sweat, he dropped the pick! It landed just inches from the angry snake. He had no choice now. Billy swung his pack back and forth to get the cobra's attention. Then suddenly he whirled it high in the air and brought it down hard, right on the cobra's head, sending it back into the far corner again.

Jumping to the floor, Billy snatched up the pick and scrambled back up on to the bed just as the cobra slithered toward him. Billy wiped his hands on his pants and went back to work on the lock. *Come on! Come on!* he thought desperately.

Just as he was about to lose hope, Billy heard the telltale *click* of the lock snapping open. With one last swipe with his pack at the snake, he jumped down and dashed out of the cell, slamming the cell door behind him.

Shoving the rest of his stuff back into his pack, he slipped it on his shoulder and took off running, hoping he had correctly remembered his dad's maps—and the way down to the slaves.

Wanting to save the batteries in his flashlight, Billy was grateful for the many torches as he made his way through the maze of caves, but they did make it more difficult to hide from the many guards patrolling the caves. Each time, he managed to duck out of sight, just in time.

As he moved from tunnel to tunnel, Billy also spotted the trip wires and other traps that had been laid, and was grimly thankful for Cobra's cruelty. For when Cobra had so coldly told him that his friends had died in a trap, he had also unknowingly warned Billy of the traps. At last, turning down yet another tunnel, he located the staircase that led to the bottom floor—where he hoped he would find the slaves . . . and his friends.

Billy was halfway down the long staircase, when he heard footsteps. He looked around, but there was nowhere to hide—and the footsteps were coming closer!

## Chapter 40

# Together Again

The guards climbed up the stone stairway and disappeared down one of the many tunnels. They never saw Billy. But had they looked up, they would have seen him, wedged against the ceiling, hands clutching one wall and feet gripping the other.

Once the guards passed, Billy dropped down and continued his journey. This was the direction the guards had come from. Hopefully that meant the slaves were down here. Billy slowly crept down a narrow tunnel. Just a few yards farther and it opened out into a large cavern. Slipping behind some fallen rocks, Billy got his first look at the slave camp.

Surrounded by a fence of bamboo spikes, he saw the slaves laboring over furnaces and piles of weapons. Guards were everywhere. Staying behind rocks, Billy made his way around the fence, looking for a way to sneak inside. He had gone nearly halfway around the enclosure when he spotted Allie.

*Allie really is alive!* he thought. *Cobra was telling the truth. And if she's alive . . . maybe Huko and Anui are too!*

Billy pulled his flashlight out of his pack. Pointing it at Allie, he clicked it on for the briefest of seconds. Making sure the guards weren't looking, he repeated this several times. At first, Allie didn't notice, but then the old woman Mohea had helped stopped her.

"Someone is trying to get your attention," the woman said kindly, pointing toward Billy.

"Really?" Allie said, looking around.

As Billy lowered his flashlight, she spotted him. *Billy!* Overjoyed, Allie made her way to the fence, careful not to attract the guards' attention.

"You're alive!" Allie said, smiling.

"And so are you!" said Billy. "Are Huko and Anui okay?"

"Yes, but we were almost killed when we tried to escape from the caves."

"What happened?"

"Anui saved us again," Allie explained. "We were running down one of the passages . . . if Anui hadn't stumbled over that trip wire and knocked Huko and me down, we would have been killed. Unfortunately, the guards heard us and we were captured. We've been here with Mohea and the others ever since. We're working on a plan to escape," she said, filling Billy in on their plan to steal the weapons.

Billy listened carefully, then said, "Allie, I know now

what Faleaka was trying to tell us. I know the answer to his riddle. It's the heart!"

"What?" Allie asked, puzzled.

By this time, Huko and Anui had also made their way over to Billy.

"The heart," Billy repeated. "It's all about our hearts. That's the answer. *'It is never seen, but always felt. It is sometimes cold, but sometimes melts. A treasure valued more than gold, by poor and rich, by young and old. Strength and power found inside . . .'"*

*"'Where worth and purpose both reside,'"* Billy and Allie finished together.

Shaking her head slightly, Allie asked, "But how can we fight Cobra with our hearts? It would make more sense if you said it was our minds. It might be possible to out-think a person and win a battle, but what does a person's heart have to do with it?"

"Each of us has our own purpose, but it starts in our hearts," Billy said, leaving Allie looking even more confused.

"Our hearts help us love others," Billy explained. "It's like this thing from the Bible my mom used to tell me about: Kindness comes from a heart filled with love, but evil comes from a heart filled with evil. God wants us to treat others with love and kindness—that's part of how we follow Him. It's what's in our hearts that makes us important. So if we will fill our hearts with love and kindness for others, then God will help us do what He created us to do. He'll help us defeat Cobra."

"First, we've got to get out of here," Allie reasoned.

"Think pineapple," Billy said with a knowing smile. "Here's what I think Faleaka had in mind . . ." and he began to explain his plan.

"You know how you made your pineapple explode?" Billy asked. "Well . . . teach the other slaves how to do it too."

Turning to Anui, Billy said, "Do you think you could make a potion that would make all of Cobra's guards fall asleep?

"Sure," said Anui, remembering the large, yellow berries.

"What about me?" asked Huko.

"You serve the guards and keep them distracted so they don't figure out what we're up to," Billy said.

"Okay," Huko agreed.

As Billy spoke, Allie saw the plan forming in her mind. "Yes," she said slowly, "we always have plenty of pineapples—the guards bring them to us for our food. But there are a few other things we'll need."

"I can bring you whatever supplies you need from the outside," Billy said.

★ ★ ★

That night, Cobra paced back and forth in his bedchamber, stopping only to stare at the ruined mural.

He held up the medallion and studied it. Then he walked over to a chair, sat down, and called for his guard.

"Yes, my lord," the man replied as he entered the room.

"Has the boy been found yet?"

The man gulped. "No, my lord, the buildings and caves have been thoroughly searched, but he has not been found."

"I want that boy found . . . now!" Cobra roared.

"Yes, my lord," said the guard, bowing and hurrying from the room.

"One way or the other, I will find you, Billy," Cobra said to himself. "And when I do, I'll make you wish you had never been born."

# Chapter 41

# A Bold Plan

All night Billy snuck in and out of the slave camp, smuggling in the needed supplies to Huko, Anui, and Allie. Allie had told him exactly what she needed to make her pineapples explode, while Anui had described a particular kind of berry. It had taken Billy quite a while to find everything.

"This is the last of it, I think," Billy said as he passed the stuff between the bars. "Do you have everything you need?"

"I hope so," Allie said. "We won't get a second chance. We've hidden enough daggers and swords for most of the slaves to have a weapon, and I've taught several of the villagers how to make the bombs. As soon as I prepare the ingredients, we can get these pineapple bombs made. Then we'll be ready . . . I hope."

"Good," Billy said, turning to leave.

"Where are you going?" Allie whispered.

"To do some scouting. I want to make sure I'm ready for Cobra."

Huko continued his chores, trying to keep the guards focused on him while Allie and Anui slipped away to work. Using charred wood from the furnaces, Allie went to work grinding charcoal, which she then mixed with crystal scrapings Billy had brought her. Once she had the ingredients just right, Allie glanced around to make sure no one was watching. She then touched a burning twig to a small bit of the powder, causing it to flash like a sparkler. A smile lit her face. Next, she gathered up the ingredients and slipped quietly through the camp. Pretending to carry wood and supplies, she passed out the ingredients to make bombs.

All through the night and into the next day, the villagers took turns making bombs—right under the guards' noses. Because they used pineapples, the guards never suspected a thing.

Meanwhile, Anui mashed the berries to extract their juice. He sweetened the juice with sugarcane and then added the mixture to some pineapple juice. Stirring it all together, he smiled to himself. *Just one sip of this and the guards will be sound asleep,* he thought.

Hours later Allie slipped over to Anui. "How's it coming?" she whispered.

"I think we're ready," Anui said, lifting a bucket of the drink.

Joining up with Huko, the two boys went to each of the guards in turn, offering to fill their cups with the fresh juice. The guards were delighted to be served by the former king.

Just as the boys had reached the last guard, two of Cobra's warriors burst into the slave camp and grabbed Huko by the arms.

"Cobra wants you," growled one of the warriors, dragging Huko out of the camp.

Allie, Anui, and the other slaves stared after Huko. It was now more important than ever that they escape.

# Chapter 42

# Cobra's Revenge

Later that night, outside Cobra's fortress, rows of torches and warriors lined a pathway leading down to a massive, black, stone platform. More than a dozen drummers pounded out a steady beat, so that it seemed as if thunder filled the air. Cobra, wearing his ceremonial blood-red robes, passed through the rows of warriors. He watched them snap to attention as he walked by, enjoying the look of fear in their eyes and their chant of "Cobra! Cobra!"

It was time to destroy the medallion.

Cobra strode toward the stone platform, carrying the medallion in his hand. Climbing the steps, he moved to the center of the platform. The chanting and drumbeats reached a deafening climax. Cobra turned to those gathered before him and signaled for silence.

"Tonight . . . we destroy our enemies!" Cobra shouted, thrusting the medallion out in front of him.

The warriors cheered wildly, as Cobra moved to one side of the platform where there stood a tall, wooden post. It had been carved with slithering cobras, and Cobra hung the medallion from the head of one of the snakes. A large pile of wood had been placed around the bottom of the post.

Cobra then walked to the other side of the platform where two guards stood. Between them, something was hidden behind a large curtain. With a flick of his arm, Cobra signaled the guards to remove the curtain. And there—with mounds of firewood piled at his feet—was Huko, tied to a thick wooden post.

"Your hopes of regaining your throne die with you this night," Cobra told the young king.

"Once I am gone, there will be another to take my place," Huko replied, sounding much more confident than he felt.

Cobra laughed. "You are the last of your line. And without the medallion, your people will crumble like dead leaves. Do you wish to speak any last words to those assembled before you?" Cobra asked mockingly.

Huko was about to refuse. What could he say to these warriors that would make any difference? But then he noticed the slaves, led by Allie, Anui, and Mohea, moving into place near the back of the assembly. Their plan must have worked! With the warriors all focused on Cobra, they had not yet been seen. So Huko began to speak.

"You may think you have won," he said, "but the battle has only begun. You thought that by destroying my father, you could remove any resistance to your tyranny. But you were wrong, just as you are wrong in thinking that my death and the destruction of the medallion will put an end to it. My people will stand up to you! For in the end, those whose hearts are kind and strong will overcome those who are dark and evil!" Huko ended, his voice ringing through the night air.

"A very nice speech," Cobra sneered. Then turning to the warriors guarding Huko, he ordered, "Light the fires!"

One of the warriors touched a torch to the wood beneath Huko, while another did the same to the pile under the medallion. The flames sputtered at first, then flared upward, licking greedily at the wood. The drums began to pound again and Cobra's men chanted, as the flames grew higher around Huko.

## Chapter 43

# Battle for Freedom

Allie had slipped into the back of the assembly with Anui and the other slaves, each of them loaded with pineapple bombs and other weapons. Seeing Huko, with flames licking at his feet, Allie stifled a scream. So this is where they had taken him! Looking around, she searched for Billy but saw no sign of him.

Huko blinked against the smoke. Coughing and sputtering, he tugged at the ropes that held him.

Her determination greater than ever before, Allie whispered to Anui, "Time to roast a snake."

Thinking Allie meant to start the attack now, Anui touched the wick of his bomb to one of the nearby torches and then hurled the pineapple toward Cobra.

Seeing Anui's pineapple go sailing by, Allie shouted, "Now!" launching the attack.

A wave of bombs rained down upon the warriors. Startled by the explosions, the terrified warriors broke ranks and scattered in fear, dropping their weapons as they ran.

Cobra stared in disbelief as a hundred whizzing pineapples flew through the air toward him. Soon realizing the bombs were harmless, he began shouting at his retreating warriors, enraged that they had tried to desert him. "Cowards!" he yelled. "Stay and fight!"

Once their bombs were gone, the slaves pulled out their stolen daggers and swords and moved toward Cobra's panicking warriors.

As soon as the attack began, Billy jumped up from his hiding place behind the platform and raced toward Huko. Reaching him, he began sawing at the ropes with his pocketknife.

"Better hurry," Huko urged, trying to sound calmer than he felt. "It is getting a little warm."

Billy sawed through the last bit of rope, and both boys jumped away from the fire.

Cobra spotted them and called to his warriors, "Get them!"

Billy ran to grab the medallion from the other post, while Huko waded into the fight, determined to help his people.

Just as Billy reached for the medallion, a fleeing warrior ran past, knocking over the post and sending the medallion flying end over end. It hit the ground with a metallic *clank!* that caused the stone to pop out and roll away.

Shoving aside the warriors who stood in his way, Cobra spotted the medallion on the ground. He started toward it and was reaching down for it when a battling warrior kicked it away. Cobra scurried after the medallion and almost had it, only to have it kicked away again. At last, his fingers closed around it. Standing with it clutched in his hand, he saw that the stone was once again missing.

★ ★ ★

Huko saw Cobra with the medallion and was about to attack when he heard Anui cry for help. Seeing his friend in trouble, Huko abandoned the medallion and ran toward Anui, snatching a sword from one of Cobra's injured guards and quickly intercepted the spear-carrying warrior advancing on his friend.

Just in time, Huko blocked the warrior's spear with his arm as Anui scrambled out of the way. With one swipe, Huko knocked the spear away. He then landed a vicious kick to the man's kidneys followed by a crushing blow to the head. Staring at the warrior for a split second, Huko then unleashed a flying tornado kick to the man's head, dropping him to the ground unconscious.

★ ★ ★

Meanwhile, Cobra searched both for the stone and for Billy, squinting through the masses of battling slaves and warriors. Finally, he spotted Billy in the distance—just as Billy spotted the stone, lying on the ground near his feet. Picking it up, he studied it for a moment, knowing that without the stone, the medallion was powerless.

Feeling Cobra's eyes upon him, Billy looked up to see him glaring at him across the battlefield. Cobra started toward Billy, but was blocked by battling warriors and slaves.

Unable to reach Billy, Cobra looked around for another way to get to him. Then, he spotted Allie only a few feet away. She was the insurance he needed to make Billy hand over the stone. Cobra shoved his way over to her and grabbed her by the arm.

"Come with me," he said coldly, dragging Allie, kicking and screaming, toward his fortress.

Seeing Cobra drag Allie away, Billy fought his way through. He saw Cobra disappear with her inside his fortress. Following quickly, Billy ran as fast as he could to catch up to them.

Bursting into the throne room, Billy found Cobra holding a terrified Allie, his deadly fanged fingernail at her throat. Seeing Billy, Cobra shoved Allie toward one of his warriors, nodding to him. Reaching up, the warrior pulled a lever in the wall, opening the Pit of Death right behind Billy's feet. The heat hit Billy like a punch.

"Did you really think you could take the medallion from me?" Cobra asked.

"I don't need the medallion," Billy replied.

"Well . . . if you don't need it, then I will take that stone off your hands in exchange for the girl."

"Don't do it, Billy," Allie pleaded. "You need the stone to stop all this."

Billy shook his head. "All right, Cobra," he said. "I'll give you the stone. But first . . . you give me Allie."

"No," Cobra smiled evilly, shaking his head. "First . . . the stone . . . or she dies."

# Chapter 44

# The Pit of Death

Billy looked down at the fiery pit, hesitating. Then he slowly reached into his pocket, pulling out a stone. Without warning, he hurled it straight at Cobra's face, hoping to catch him off guard.

But with the lightning quick speed of a striking cobra, Cobra snatched the stone out of the air. Tossing it to the ground, he glared at Billy, fury filling his face. "The real stone," he snarled.

Billy drew the stone out of his pocket and held it toward Cobra in his outstretched hand. "Come and get it," he said.

Cobra stepped toward Billy, his hand reaching out to take the stone. Just as his fingers were about to close over it, Billy dropped the stone to the ground. Swinging Faleaka's staff as hard as he could, Billy attacked. But Cobra was too quick. For a moment, he allowed Billy to attack, his blows bouncing off him uselessly. Then Cobra smiled icily, shaking his head. Raising his fanged fingers high, he moved toward Billy.

Edging slowly backward, Billy moved around the edge of the pit. Cobra hesitated and then leapt over the corner of the pit, landing in front of him. Billy attacked again. Swinging the staff with all his might, he caught Cobra behind the knees. Knocking him off balance, Billy moved in to attack again, but Cobra's warrior stepped between them, so that Billy's throw hit him instead.

Cobra shoved the man out of the way, "You fool," he said, swinging wildly at Billy with his poisoned fingers.

Billy ducked, Cobra's blow narrowly missing him. But as Cobra's arm came around, Billy grabbed it and pushed it upward in a sweeping motion toward his neck, causing one of Cobra's poisoned nails to slice his own throat. Cobra froze, waiting for the agonizing pain to send him into convulsions—waiting for the death he had inflicted upon countless others. But moments passed and nothing happened.

An evil grin spread across Cobra's face. "Apparently my skin wasn't broken," he laughed.

But as Billy stared at the welt on Cobra's neck, a tiny drop of blood appeared, quickly followed by several more. Now that the wound had started bleeding, Billy knew it would only be a matter of time. Cobra remained unaware of the blood that seeped from the wound. Since the scratch had been shallow, it was taking the poison longer to reach his bloodstream.

Cobra started toward Billy, determined to throw him into the Pit of Death. But then he felt something wet trickle down his throat. He touched his hand to his neck and pulled it back again, staring down in horror at the blood on it. Suddenly, Cobra grabbed his throat as the liquid fire of the poison raced through his body.

As Cobra started to fall back into the pit, Billy ran forward and grabbed hold of the medallion. But as the two struggled for possession, Cobra's feet slipped on the floor and he slid backward over the edge of the pit. Billy held on tight to the medallion, bracing himself as Cobra plunged downward before stopping abruptly. The only thing keeping him from falling to his death was Billy's grip on the medallion.

Cobra's mind filled with rage over his own stupidity. How could he have allowed himself to be bested by a mere child? He tried to swing his leg up to the edge of the pit. But as convulsions began to rip through his body, his grip weakened, and he slipped further, his weight pulling Billy closer to the edge of the pit.

"Billy! Let go!" Allie screamed. "Let go of the medallion!"

But Billy refused. If he let go, the medallion would be lost forever.

"Billy! Please!" Allie threw off the warrior holding her and ran to Billy, grabbing his legs and pulling backward. "Let go! It's not worth your life!" Allie cried as Billy slipped closer to the edge and certain death.

"It's my whole life," Billy said.

"No, Billy! Remember what Faleaka told you—it was never about the medallion. It's about the heart, remember? Let it go, Billy! You're slipping."

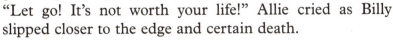

Billy slipped still closer, half of him now dangling over the edge.

"You don't need the medallion," Allie screamed.

Staring eye to eye with Cobra, Billy made his decision. He opened his fingers and . . . let go. Then he watched in horror as Cobra fell backward, screaming, into the flames.

Cobra's warrior grabbed Billy's legs and, to Allie's astonishment, hauled Billy to his feet, pulling him away from the edge.

"Allie!" Billy yelled, wrapping her in a huge hug.

Looking very relieved, the warrior turned to them and said, "He did not have a kind heart."

Billy nodded, as he reached down and picked up the stone, returning it to his pocket.

★ ★ ★

Outside the slaves had defeated the warriors, and as Billy and Allie entered the area, the villagers cheered. Huko and Anui came running, relieved to see their friends still alive. Huko and Anui lifted Billy on their shoulders as the villagers cheered their hero.

For the first time in his life, Huko was happy to give someone else the credit. He had finally realized the true meaning of what it meant to be a king. Thanks to Billy and Allie, he would have a chance to show his people that he was worthy of being their ruler.

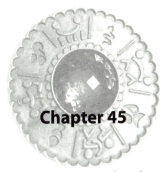

## Chapter 45

# Time to Celebrate

*The next night . . .*

Billy, Allie, Huko, Anui, and all the others had returned to Aumakua Island. And, just as Huko had promised, Faleaka's body was carefully laid to rest in the gardens near his hut. The villagers brought bundles of bright, tropical flowers and placed them over his grave. With the ceremony completed, the kids were left alone to say good-bye to their friend.

"Thank you, wise Faleaka, for showing me the path I desperately needed to find. I have not been a very good king up to now. But I promise you—and the Great King—I will serve my people in kindness," Huko said solemnly.

"Rest in peace, Faleaka," Billy added. "I now know my worth is not found in things outside of me but was placed inside of me by God himself."

"Thank you, Faleaka, for helping me to understand that I do have a purpose and that no one is an accident to God," Allie whispered, a tear sliding down her cheek.

"Good-bye, good friend," said Anui simply.

★ ★ ★

The four then returned to the village—and to the biggest feast any of them had ever seen. It was time to celebrate.

Music and laughter filled the air, mingling with the scent of sweet-smelling flowers and mouth-watering foods. The women moved joyfully through a traditional dance. As they finished, a small boy ran up to Huko and whispered something in his ear.

Huko smiled and stood.

"It is time for the presentation of the feast!" he announced.

Anui walked proudly out of his hut, followed by two other villagers carrying a delicious-looking roasted pig on a huge platter. Anui smiled as everyone cheered his creation.

Taking the first bite, Huko smiled. Knowing his friend's love for food, he said, "Anui, I declare you to be head chef for our entire village!"

A bit later, an elderly lady—the one Mohea had saved—bowed before Huko and began to serve him.

"No," Huko said, standing and giving her his chair. "I will serve you," Huko told the astonished woman.

"You remind me of your father," the woman said, patting him on the cheek.

"Thank you," Huko said, thinking this was the greatest compliment he had ever received.

## Chapter 46

# The Staff

The next day, Huko and Anui walked with Billy and Allie around the island. Stopping to rest near a waterfall, Billy stared out at the jungle around him.

"You know we're here for good," Allie said, resigning herself to a life in the past.

Billy nodded, leaning against his staff. *Wait!* he thought. *The staff . . .*

"Allie, I've got an idea," Billy said, a gleam in his eye as he stood up. "Follow me, you guys."

"Where are we going?" Allie asked.

"You'll see," Billy said. "I'm still a little fuzzy on how this time travel thing works, but if my hunch is right . . . we need to find that man-shaped rock."

For the next half hour, Billy led Allie, Huko, and Anui

on a quest, searching for a large rock that was shaped like a man—the one they had hidden behind to escape Cobb's men that fateful day.

At last, Billy spotted the rock. "There it is!" he shouted, pulling Allie forward. Huko and Anui followed close behind.

"What are we doing here?" Allie asked. "Wait a minute. Isn't this is the spot where we found the medallion?"

Billy nodded, pulled his trowel from his pack, and dropped to his knees. Moving aside a small boulder, he began to dig.

"But, Billy," Allie protested, "the medallion can't be here. It went over the cliff with Cobra."

"Just trust me," Billy said, then he added, "and help me dig!"

Soon, Billy heard the familiar *clink!* of metal hitting metal. Eyes wide with anticipation, Billy tossed the trowel aside and finished digging with his fingers. At last, he pulled out the bundle of blue cloth. Folding back the fabric, he saw it—the medallion!

Allie, Huko, and Anui stared in amazement.

"How did you know it would be here?" Allie asked.

Billy shrugged and said, "Faleaka's walking stick. I mean, I brought his back, but he still had his here too."

Holding the medallion in one hand, Billy used his other hand to reach into his pocket and pull out the stone. As before, the stone glowed brightly and jumped from his hand into the medallion, sealing itself into place.

Billy stared at the medallion for a moment. Then, leaning over, he started to place it around Huko's neck, but Huko stopped him.

"You keep it," said Huko. "It's what you've been look-ing for."

Billy shook his head. "I've always had what I've been looking for. It was just . . . buried inside me," he shrugged, grinning.

Once again, Billy leaned over to put the medallion around Huko's neck . . . and this time Huko did not object.

Allie smiled at them both.

"I will leave the medallion here for you," Huko promised.

* * *

Returning to the village, Huko called for his people to gather around. Holding up the now restored medallion, he said, "We must hang this in the center of our village as a reminder that everyone is of great worth and that our hearts must be filled with kindness."

The villagers cheered, hugging each other. After all these years and after all the hardships, everything was at last as it should be.

Huko raised his hand to quiet the villagers.

"It took me a long time, but I have finally learned that my father's words were true. Our value comes from  the Great King, the One who created us—*each of us*—with a purpose. We are each royal, because we are children of the Great King," Huko declared. "And we show our royalty by how we honor our Father and how we honor each other."

Turning to Billy and Allie, Huko said to them, "You have done so much for my people . . . our people. I feel I should give you something in return. What would you like? Name anything and it is yours. Thanks to the medallion, I have the power to grant it."

"Allie and I just want to go home," Billy replied.

"Very well. I thank you, my future many-times-great-grandson, for saving *our* island," Huko said, bowing humbly to Billy.

Billy looked at the medallion resting against Huko's heart. After all that had happened, it was hard to believe they were really going back home. Turning to Allie, he asked, "Ready?"

Allie nodded. "Good-bye. I'm going to miss you both," Allie said, hugging Huko and then Anui.

"Okay," Billy said, "let's go save my dad."

Reaching down, Billy grabbed Faleaka's staff in both hands, holding it as if preparing for a fight. Allie laid one hand on Billy's arm and gave a small wave to the villagers with the other.

"I wish them back home where they belong," Huko said.

In a flash of blue light, Billy and Allie disappeared.

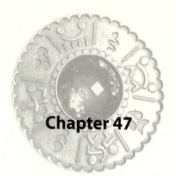

**Chapter 47**

# A Few Things Have Changed

Billy and Allie materialized inside Billy's home. As soon as Billy felt his feet hit the smooth, tiled surface of the floor, he swung Faleaka's staff as hard as he could, smashing  it into Kalani's chin and sending him reeling. Swinging back again, he caught Makala squarely in his large stomach, doubling him over in pain.

Both men collapsed to the floor in agony.

"Billy!" Dr. Stone shouted in alarm. "What's going on? Please tell me that is not what you wanted to show me with that staff! Why did you attack them?"

Hearing his father's voice, Billy barely managed to stop himself from hitting Makala a second time. Staring in disbelief, Billy stammered, "I . . . I thought . . . they were part of Cobra's gang."

"*Whose* gang?" Dr. Stone asked, puzzled by Billy's words.

"Cobra's . . . I mean . . . Cobb's gang . . ." Billy said, his voice trailing off.

"Whose . . . what? *What* gang?" Kalani asked, rubbing his chin.

"Young Billy," Makala said, casting a disgusted look back at his partner, "I can assure you 'tis not open season on archaeologists."

Billy and Allie looked at each other in amazement.

"I am . . . I am so sorry," Billy apologized.

"I think a few things have changed, Billy," Allie said.

"If this is some game you two are playing, I don't get it," said Dr. Stone, helping his battered assistants to their feet.

"Sorry, guys," Billy apologized again. "I thought you were trying to hurt my dad."

"Why on earth would you think that?" Makala asked.

"It's a long story," Allie chimed in.

"Dad," Billy said, turning to his father, "I think I know where you can find the medallion."

★ ★ ★

A short time later, after Billy and Allie had led Dr. Stone to the other side of the island, they knelt in the dirt in front of the large stone that was strangely shaped like a man. Dr. Stone stared at it in amazement.

"It really is shaped like a man," he whispered. "Just as the legend said. I had begun to think that even it wasn't real."

Filling with hope and excitement, Dr. Stone lifted up the large stone that Billy had pointed out to him. Digging carefully in the dirt beneath it, he felt the telltale scrape of metal against metal. Throwing the shovel aside, his excitement growing, he dug around the area with his fingers until the archeologist pulled the cloth-wrapped medallion out of the ground.

"King Huko's emblem," Dr. Stone whispered, carefully removing the cloth. Inside the cloth and tightly wrapped around the medallion, he found a note, carefully preserved by the stone's power. Dr. Stone read it aloud.

*Dear Billy,*

He shot his son a startled look.

*I am an old man now, ready to pass my kingship on to my son. I have had little reason to use the medallion over the years. The Great King has been good to us. For that reason, and because I wish to remove temptation from those to come who might have evil designs on the stone's power, I have decided to keep my promise to you and rebury the medallion in the spot where my father placed it for safekeeping so long ago.*

*I do this, knowing that one day you will retrieve it.*

*Please find a safe place for the medallion, one where the people of your time may look upon, but not touch, the wonderful treasure entrusted to my father by the Great King. I trust that you will know where the medallion belongs.*

*Your many times great-grandfather,*
*Huko*

"Leave it to Huko to call himself 'many times great,'" Allie laughed.

"I have a feeling the two of you have quite a tale to tell," Dr. Stone said, staring at the medallion in awe.

Billy couldn't stop smiling. "You've found your treasure, Dad."

Dr. Stone lowered the medallion, a shadow crossing his face. "No, Billy," he said, his voice filled with sadness and regret. "*We've* found a great treasure, but I've always had an even greater treasure . . . you. I'm sorry I seemed to have forgotten that," he said, pulling Billy into his arms and hugging him tightly. "Your mom would be so proud of you."

**Chapter 48**

# The *Real* Medallion

Over the next few days and weeks, Billy and Allie discovered that many things had changed on their island.

Allie thought perhaps that she was most grateful for the changes at the orphanage. A few days after they had returned to their own time, Allie told Billy, "Come on, I want to show you something."

The two friends rode Billy's dirt bike to the orphanage. "You're finally letting me see where you live?" Billy asked.

"Well," Allie said simply, "now, it's worth seeing."

Allie took him inside and showed him around. The changes that Allie had discovered upon her return still amazed her. The battered receptionist's desk was now a beautiful, wooden table filled with flowers. The staff was now warm and caring, as were the girls who lived there.

The drab walls and floors had been replaced with

warm colors and soft, braided rugs. The walls were filled with pictures made by the children themselves. There was even a playroom. Allie's own room was filled with sturdy, new furniture, a soft bed, and colorful quilts.

As the two friends started to leave, Allie said, "Oh, wait! I almost forgot. There's just one more thing I have to show you." Pointing to a plaque near the door, Billy was astonished to learn that his father—once again a world-renowned archeologist—was a major contributor to the orphanage.

"Well, now you've seen my home," Allie stated.

"So you're not going to run away?" Billy asked.

"Absolutely not!" Allie laughed. "There are a lot of girls here who could use some kindness."

Billy and Allie walked back to his bike.

"Now I want to show *you* something," Billy told her excitedly.

Driving through the city center, they admired more of the changes that had occurred, thanks to their trip through time. The buildings were neat and freshly painted. More important, *Cobb Enterprises, Inc.,* was no longer plastered all over everything.

At the edge of town, they passed a run-down, tourist-trap. The sign over the ragged entrance read: *Cobra Snake Farm.* Sitting out front was Cobb himself. Sporting a scraggly beard, he was shabbily dressed in a dirty, flowered shirt and torn jeans. His hair, no longer sleek, was long and tangled. Instead of running the city, he was a broken man, in a rickety chair, running a pitiful little snake farm.

A little farther down the road, Billy stopped his bike in front of the island's museum. What had once been a

run-down joke of a museum was now a beautiful building.
Three tall arches framed its stucco front. Elegant double
doors stood on either side of a glass-enclosed bulletin
board that told visitors about the current displays.

Billy and Allie stepped inside and strolled through the
beautiful black and white marble interior filled with native
artifacts in gleaming cases. Near the center of the room,
Billy stopped to study Faleaka's hawk-topped walking stick
resting in a case. The plaque read:

## STAFF OF FALEAKA,
## THE GREAT WISE MAN

All around them were cases filled with artifacts—most
of them dug up by Billy's father and his teams. There was
even a small glass case that held Mohea's journal.

"We really did change things when we went back in
time," Allie said.

"Yeah," Billy agreed. "Now come look at this," he
said, pointing over to the grandest display of all. Behind
thick security glass, under a web of laser beams, the royal
medallion rested on a plush, velvet cushion.

Billy and Allie looked at it, each thinking back over all
their adventures.

"Do you ever miss it?" Allie asked. "Having the
medallion?"

Billy stared thoughtfully at the medallion, then slowly
shook his head. "No," he said, starting to smile. "Because
now I know that my heart is my medallion, and . . ."

". . . and the Great King is the stone," Allie added with
a smile.

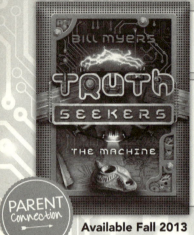

# A NEW SERIES FROM

accomplished writer and film director **BILL MYERS**

Twin siblings Jake and Jennifer have just lost their mother and are not thrilled about moving to Israel to stay with their seldom seen archaeologist dad. They don't yet understand how "all things work together for good to those who love God." But they will when a machine their father invented points them to the Truth.

**Available Fall 2013**

---

## A New & Exciting Adventure

When a cranky, video game-loving city kid named Beamer has to spend the summer on a farm with his country cousin Bash, he suspects it's gonna stink—and not just because there's a pig involved. But, through Bash's zany adventures with his "Fishin' and Farmin' book" (The Bible) it just might lead Beamer to the coolest Discovery of all.

**BASH and the Pirate Pig**

by BURTON W. COLE
illustrations by TOM BANCROFT

**Available Fall 2013**